A
SONG
FOR
KATY SHAYNE

A
SONG
FOR
KATY SHAYNE

JIM FUSILLI

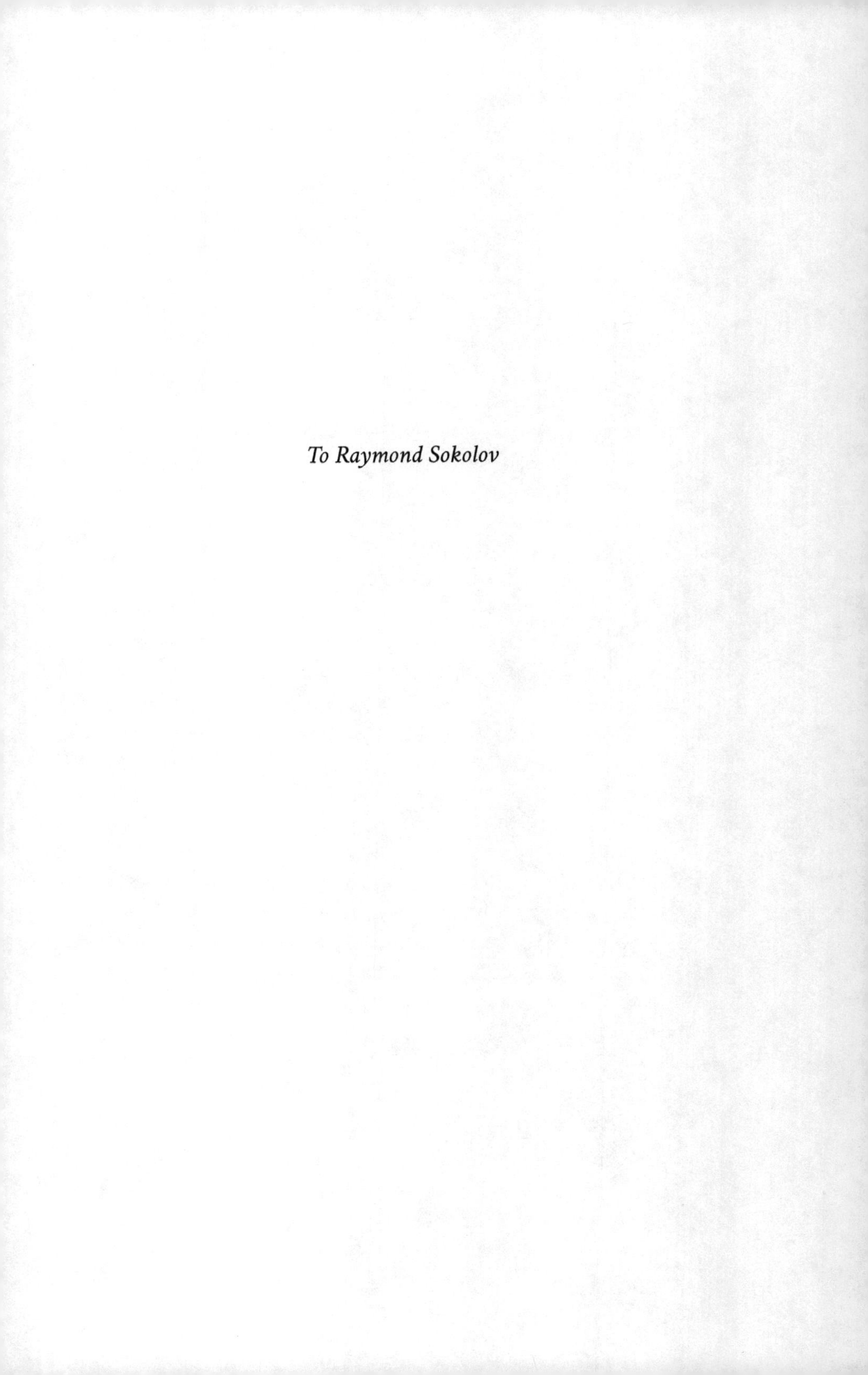

To Raymond Sokolov

Praise for A Song for Katy Shayne

"A fast-paced, hardboiled tale with a warm heart. Jim Fusilli's protagonist is a man of integrity and passion, dedicated to music, underdogs, hard work, food, and the love of his life. It's impossible not to root for him."—Howard Fishman, author of *To Anyone Who Ever Asks: The Life, Music, and Mystery of Connie Converse*

"In *A Song for Katy Shayne*, Jim Fusilli has crafted a compelling blend of the world of journalism with the world of music. Fusilli brings us behind the scenes where we see for ourselves the seamier side of the music business. He's created a fascinating character in Jack Fiorello, a music critic on the cusp of being put out to pasture, who's drawn into a decades old suicide of a young, up-and-coming folk singer. Fiorello knows a good story when he sees one, as does Fusilli, who takes the reader on a wild ride, as he tries to get a handle on why a talented young woman might have taken her own life."—Charles Salzberg, a 3-time Shamus Award nominee, is a former magazine journalist and author of *Man on the Run.*

"Blending an evocative plot and an unrivaled understanding of the music industry, Jim Fusilli has crafted in *A Song for Katy Shayne* a mystery that captivates from start to finish and features one of the most unusual protagonists you'll likely ever meet.

"The story centers on aging, laid-off, music critic Jack Fiorello, who finds himself investigating the death of an aspiring, openly gay folk singer named Katy Shayne. According to the NYPD, Shayne committed suicide in 1977 by throwing herself off the roof of a Manhattan high-rise. The deeper Fiorello digs, however, the more he comes to be convinced otherwise. His journey to uncover the truth will lead him into the ghostly past of New York's once-burgeoning folk scene, and to the unearthing of secrets never meant to be found.

"Fusilli's writing talents, shaped by his many years as rock-and-pop critic for the *Wall Street Journal*, shine through on every page. His prose is sharp and heartfelt. With its richly authentic atmospherics, unforgettable characters, and a plot that will keep you guessing, *A Song for Katy Shayne* is a must-read for anyone who appreciates vintage music and a unique story well-told."—David Freed, Pulitzer Prize-winning former reporter for *the Los Angeles Times* and author of the bestselling Cordell Logan mystery series

Chapter One

He woke slowly. As fragments of his dreams vanished, clarity came in a rush. It was his birthday.

He cleared his throat. "Molly?"

She was already gone. He wondered if she had kissed his forehead before she left. Her perfume was still in the air.

He scratched through wayward gray hair. On his nightstand, a water bottle. His fingers covered its Wu-Tang logo as he took a lukewarm sip.

His bones crackled as he stood. "I ache in the places where I used to play," wrote Leonard Cohen. Exactly so.

Clutching the waistband of his scotch-plaid pajama bottoms, he padded barefoot toward the bathroom. As he passed through the living room, he saw on the kitchen counter a cupcake with a single unlit candle.

"Happiest, young man," read Molly's note. "Are you available tonight? Say yes."

Yes, until 11 p.m. when he had to be in Williamsburg for an unannounced midnight set by D'Angelo, a musician he admired without reservation. Questlove had texted the tip.

He ran his finger across the mocha icing.

What the hell, he thought as he hoisted up on the high stool. He ate the cupcake in three bites.

The November chill prickling through his gray T, Jack left the counter to nudge the thermostat up a few degrees.

Then, walking the cupcake wrapper to the kitchen trashcan, he was warmed by memories: Last night at the Bowery Ballroom; oh, she was so superb. She came out burning, her neon-blue pantsuit glowing in the spotlight, mustard streaks glistening in her firetruck-red hair. Adding a touch of sandpaper to her crystal voice, she led her band through her familiar and obscure numbers, funking up a few, bending others, all the while giving the crisscrossing music a delightful ticklishness. Late in the set, she stepped back to let the crowd take over the vocals. Dotted with lights from a mirror ball, they were still singing with gusto when she left the stage. Later, Jack memorialized what he witnessed, notebook on his thigh, on an icy stoop in SoHo.

Happy then, happy again, Jack plopped back into bed and found the warm spot where he had lain.

"It's 2018, isn't it?" he asked the ceiling. "I'm sixty-five."

When he was a kid, 65 was the end. If a man managed to live that long.

"I've managed to live that long," thought Jack, who wanted another mocha cupcake.

He reviewed his day. He had already passed on a listening event: a new Dylan album, out early next year. He couldn't bear mixing with the straining-to-be-hip, look-at-me trade press, who, while attacking the buffet like the Simpsons at a kegger, insulted the art and the artists as the new music played. "I'll catch up," Jack wrote when declining the invitation. The press kit was in his little home office. On the album cover was a marble bust on display at the Vatican of an old man from first century B.C. With hollow eyes and long ears, the old man was withered and neglected. Expressions of unwinding time hadn't much changed in 2,100 years.

Hands cupped behind his head, Jack asked: I can't make time for Bob Dylan? In his weekly column, Jack preferred to focus on emerging artists and what was happening far from the mainstream. But history mattered. Context mattered. From Bob Dylan, Jack learned that nothing began when you thought it did. Dylan traveled along and understood what he had seen. He had shaken free.

Jack had met Dylan once, briefly, at a rehearsal for an all-star thing in his honor at Madison Square Garden. It was an uneventful exchange.

He realized he was eager to hear the new album. Dylan had written new material, his Sinatra phase done. Jack glanced at the clock on Molly's nightstand. He could make it to the studio in time.

The cupcake would serve as breakfast. He went off to shave and shower.

Dressed in jeans, he wriggled into a heavy pullover as he entered his office. Opening his email, he saw a request from Brussels to sign off on the European edition's edit of his story that had been in the morning's U.S. paper. Brussels had cut about 100 words for space. Tighter was better.

Fighting a crosstown gust of wind, Jack turned onto Chambers Street, head down, hands buried in his pockets. He slalomed around a UPS driver who, shoving a loaded hand truck, wore earmuffs that matched his uniform. Jack said hello to the man who sold music from West Africa from a tabletop, even in the slapping cold. The man brightened at the sight of a familiar customer.

"Sir," said the man hurriedly, his words clipped, his accent thick, "I have an excellent thing for you. Very excellent."

"Running, Femi," Jack replied with a wave. "Later, maybe."

He bought a copy of *The New National Observer* and took it underground. Jack was still pumped to see his byline in print even after all these years. He savored a minor glow of contentment. Self-satisfaction was a foe to the creative mind, but he enjoyed the acknowledgment that he existed. Said so right there in black-on-white.

Soon, the uptown train rattled into the station. Rush hour over, he found a seat and shook open the broadsheet. He saw an echo in the second and third grafs. A flat verb. One day, he would get it right. Readers deserve no less.

At 14th Street, he crossed the platform to wait for an uptown local. The scent of the muck down between the ties soiled the air. A clock affixed to the overhead beams was off by four hours. Somewhere deep in the underground maze, someone played a pipa for loose change.

Red Moleskine notebook and *The Observer* under his arm, Jack peered down the cold tunnel: no train in sight, no grinding wheels. To pass the time, he slipped into his imagination, an act so easily achieved that it took no effort. Soon, Jimi Hendrix was standing right over there, his Strat in a gig bag on his shoulder. Thelonious Monk was waiting for the uptown express near a steel pillar; lost in the whirlwind of his genius, he stared nowhere and noticed everything. Sister Rosetta Tharpe wore a white fox stole. She hummed a mournful gospel tune. Jack watched to see if the musicians greeted each other.

Long before Jack had met a single artist of achievement, he imagined himself as a bystander in their world. Such fantasies helped dull childhood anxiety, but at the same time a philosophy unfolded and soon, as if inherently, he understood how he would proceed: as a chronicler, an advocate, a missionary. A conduit between the art and the people who could appreciate it. In the quiet of his boyhood bedroom, he chatted with countless musicians then well beyond his reach.

A garbled announcement brought Jack back to where he had been. Then his iPhone buzzed. A call from Lee Reinhard, the Arts Today editor at *The Observer*, had gone directly to voicemail. "Who's dead?" said Jack to no one. The only time Reinhard called was when a musician died suddenly, and Jack had to write a critical analysis known at *The Observer* as IMs, shorthand for In Memoriam. A miserable assignment, Jack often had less than an hour to balance his feelings of loss with the need to create in a short space a sense of why the artist had been significant.

But Reinhard was asking Jack to lunch. In his voice message, he apologized for the last-minute invitation. He thought he had sent an email over the weekend. "Let me know if you're available. I'll come over to the Odeon." An American bistro, woody with banquettes, only a short walk from Jack and Molly's.

Jack was surprised by the invitation. He rarely socialized with his *Observer* colleagues; when he saw them outside of the Varick Street office, it was at a funeral or a memorial service. Never a birthday celebration. And Jack liked that Reinhard chose the Odeon. When Jack was a college kid wandering around Manhattan and soaking up all the atmosphere he could, he would stop at the Odeon and have a beer at the bar. Not a ton of musicians hung there, but he saw David Byrne once or twice and Tom Verlaine and also the guys from the "Saturday Night Live" band. One night he left the Mudd Club after a late set by Arthur Russell and was wandering through Tribeca when he felt a need to pee. There were alleys everywhere, but he looked for a bar or restaurant. Lights on in the Odeon, Jack walked in and found John Belushi frying burgers in the kitchen.

Jack texted Reinhard's secretary. "OK. 1 p.m."

The new Dylan would have to wait.

Shown to a four-seater topped with white butcher paper, he ordered an iced tea and, as he squeezed a lemon wedge, saw Reinhard exiting a taxi, returning his company-issued credit card to his wallet.

Tall, fit from his daily bouts of racquetball, Reinhard seemed harried as he approached the table. A ride along Canal Street could take forever, with jolting stops and lurching starts, yet he wasn't but a few minutes late. Nevertheless, he apologized as he removed his trench coat and scarf. He wielded his authority lightly.

They ordered immediately: Reinhard the three-egg Roquefort omelet, Jack the *moules frites.*

Reinhard hadn't mentioned his birthday, but Jack figured he was settling in. He looked like he needed to catch his breath.

"This is nice," Jack said. "Thanks for coming across town."

Reinhard unfurled his napkin and placed it across his lap.

"Jack, I have to tell you something." He put his elbows on the table. "We're making a change. Rock and Pop is leaving Arts Today."

Jack wasn't sure he understood.

"It's going to belong to News."

"News will manage critics?" Jack asked. Arts criticism was opinion, not hard reporting. It belonged with Editorial.

The waitress placed Reinhard's steaming coffee on the table.

"There aren't going to be any rock critics," Reinhard said as she departed. "Rock will be covered as lifestyle. Commerce and lifestyle. Reaction, not analysis."

Stunned, Jack fumbled a comment. "How could this… That's ridiculous."

"There's nothing I could do. Upstairs monitors traffic. It's nothing more than that. Clicks. Just clicks."

"I thought I was getting clicks."

He nodded. "But a story on a new band from the Arkansas backwoods or Reykjavik or some such doesn't draw the kind of traffic—"

"Yeah, OK. I'm not writing about household names, but—"

"Apparently, readers like what they know—"

"But isn't that the point? The buzz begins with us. How many times have we talked about this, Lee? That *The Observer* shouldn't follow the pack."

Reinhard sipped his coffee and said, "Look, Jack, I get it. But it's out of my hands." He mentioned Gideon Bibbish, the editor of the Editorial page. "I put up a fight, but…I'm sorry."

Jack shook his head almost imperceptibly. "This is unbelievable."

"TV is going too, for what it's worth."

"So now I'm reporting to News? I'm… No, wait—" Aghast, Jack blanched. "There isn't going to be a rock-and-pop critic."

Reinhard held up a hand. "We have an idea. And it's not bad."

The waitress set down the pot of steaming mussels. The briny scent wafted toward Jack, who, dizzy, was unaware his meal had arrived.

"We want you to continue to do the IMs," Reinhard said as she twisted a pepper grinder above his omelet.

Jack groped for composure. "The Dead Rock Star beat."

"I looked at your list. There are still sixty-seven names on it."

A few years ago, Jack was asked to create a list of rock and pop musicians he thought worthy of an *Observer* IM. The original list tallied about 100.

"I know you don't like to do them in advance, but you can write them now. Or when you take the buyout, you can do them as a free-lancer."

"Hold on. Lee, you buried the lede." Jack pointed at him with a tiny fork. "What you're saying is not only am I no longer the rock-and-pop critic, I'm no longer employed."

Reinhard grimaced. "I'm sorry. Yes, the buyout. HR is messengering a letter to you. You know what the package is, don't you?"

One week's salary for each year of service. He worked the simplest math: His 37 years equaled 37 weeks at full salary.

"Jack?"

"What about medical?"

"Retiree medical, yes."

Now I'm a fuckin' retiree, Jack thought. "Jesus Christ, Lee. You're cold-cocking the hell out of me."

"I am sorry," he said. "But you had to see it coming, given your age."

"I saw nothing coming," Jack replied. "I'm doing the work. What else is there? I don't pay attention if it's not music." Jack looked at the mussels, but he had no appetite. "When is my last day?"

"Stay on 'til year's end."

"So, a few more columns on living musicians. Active living musicians."

"If you'd like. Yes."

Jack slid his chair away from the table. "I need a minute," he said, his voice cracking as he stood.

The restrooms were down a steep flight of stairs. Shaking, Jack held tightly onto the banister. When he stepped into the empty men's room, he stared into the mirror. He didn't see someone who was disposable. He didn't see a retiree. He saw himself, no different than he had been 10 minutes ago, but entirely and irreparably altered. He was out of a job he loved and had defined him for most of his adult life. Jack couldn't begin to comprehend the ramifications. He shuddered and felt ashamed. He thought he might cry. He hadn't cried since Lou Reed died. Lou, who loved to talk Chandler, Cain, Goodis, Thompson. Lou, who sent barbed notes to Jack.

When Jack returned to the table, Reinhard was wrapping up a call. As he put down his phone, he mentioned the paper's TV critic by name. "I have to see her now."

Thanks for making me your priority, Jack thought.

Reinhard said, "No one wanted this, Jack. You have to understand that."

"Tell me something. Did anyone mention the work?"

Reinhard frowned in confusion.

"Did anybody say: 'You know, this guy is a pretty good critic. He works his ass off. Nobody is doing what he does for us.' Did anybody say anything like that?"

Reinhard said, "No. But it wouldn't have made any difference. It's not your talent. Or diligence. It's policy."

Jack's heart raced; his mind spun.

"Seriously. Would you take a job with News if you couldn't write as a critic?"

Jack G. Fiorello was done at *The Observer*. He could feel his spirit leave his body. Soon, he was empty.

"I think I have to tell my wife," he managed.

Chapter Two

Bereft, thoughts colliding, Jack mistakenly took a West Side subway to midtown, though Molly was all the way over on the East Side. Below New York, he indulged no fantasies. He did not see Ella Fitzgerald, Buddy Holly or Howlin' Wolf. Zombie-walking through Grand Central, he dropped the Dylan press kit into a trash can guarded by a young soldier prepared for terror.

Out in the bitter wind, the tips of his ears bright red, people did not merely look through him. They had no idea he was there as he straggled across town.

Geo Strategic Communications shared a 14th-floor suite with the Water Solution, a non-profit that helped sub-Saharan Africans find, distribute and protect clean drinking water. The receptionist, a young woman from Kenya, buzzed him in. She was new to Jack. He rarely visited. GSC was Molly's thing, as *The New National Observer* had been his.

"Can you tell Mrs. Fiorello I'm here?"

She smiled politely, professionally, and asked his name.

"Ah, you are the journalist," she said after he replied.

Jack could only manage a wane smile. "Please tell her it's not an emergency. I can wait."

Removing his leather coat, he took a seat next to a table with copies of the Water Solution's annual report, *the Economist, the Chronicle of Philanthropy, the Stanford Social Innovation Review.* He placed his red notebook on his lap. The heating system issued a gentle hum. Jack closed his eyes. There was Reinhard. He flagged a cab, then shook Jack's hand outside the Odeon.

Goodbye, Jack. Let us know.

Molly wore a navy pantsuit and an ivory blouse, as befit a president and CEO. In business mode, she marched efficiently toward her husband.

She was pleased to see him. "What's going on?"

"Oh, I'm just…I'm a little disjointed." He pointed over her shoulder toward her office.

She stepped aside to let him pass. She said, "Thank you, Njeri."

Jack said, "Thank you, Njeri."

GSC had five full-time employees, all of whom worked in cubicles. Irie Dunbar, her tri-lingual admin, was perpetually effervescent. Jack was relieved to find she was away from her desk. He couldn't bear such good cheer.

He asked if they could use the conference room. Its motif was a soothing blue, reminiscent of fresh, clean water. Jack dropped his notebook and coat on a chair. Beyond the ceiling-to-floor window, the United Nations and the East River were poised to eavesdrop.

Molly settled at the head of the table as Jack began to pace.

"Molly, I'm fired from *The National Observer*."

"Oh, Jack. No." A second earlier, she expected they would talk about his birthday. She was about to ask if he enjoyed the cupcake.

She shook her head in disbelief. "Why?"

He explained.

"So you're not really fired. You've been offered a buyout."

"'Offered' isn't right. It's not like I have a choice. I'm being forced out."

"Your skills translate. Did they offer you a lateral position?"

"Please, Molly. I need the feels. I'm shook. Look." He held out a quaking hand.

"I'm sorry. I know what it means to you." She touched his cheek. "You don't have to be brave,"

He slumped against the table. "Can you believe it? 'Jack, get out.'"

He told her about the Dead Rock Star beat.

"Oh, you hate that."

"I hate that. In my end days, I'm surrounded by the ghosts of people who haven't made any worthy music in decades."

"They loved your Tom Petty write-up, right?"

Jack was upset when he wrote about Petty. His column reflected his emotional state. Petty was still working at an admirable level. As he wrote, he was grieving for the loss of what could have been.

"Reinhard loved everything," Jack said. "And nothing. I'm out."

"Do you want to talk to Suzi?"

GSC's outside counsel. Suzi was a shark.

Jack shrugged.

"Tell me again. You can do sixty-seven columns at salary now versus what you'd get for sixty-seven columns at a freelancer's rate?"

"Freelancing is a better deal."

"I'm not worrying about the money. What's best for you?"

"There's no 'best,' babe—"

"As your employer, they own the copyright on all your columns. Let Suzi talk to them, make them part of the exit package. You could put together a collection."

"Old columns by a bought-out retiree."

"A unique, highly personal overview of the past four decades in rock-and-pop history by one of America's most respected journalists."

Frustrated, Molly ran her hand through her hair. Now, she began to pace, passing through streams of afternoon sunlight. "It's so abrupt," she said, "and terribly unfair."

They both knew Jack's time had to end one day. Already, *The Observer* had stopped using him on webcasts. Even if he felt at least a decade younger, he looked 65. His eyebrows were gray. He had liver spots on the back of his hands. But he and Molly assumed there would be a transition period. Jack G. might do two columns a month. Eventually, a graceful exit would be proposed. He would be Critic Emeritus. An *éminence grise*. Jack considered himself helpful. Why ignore someone in need?

Molly stared at a long, empty barge on the cold, gray-green river. Seagulls circled and pecked.

Jack sank into a chair. "I thought he came across town to celebrate my birthday. How oblivious am I?"

She turned. "I really am sorry."

"Me too."

"Promise me you won't make it worse."

"How could it be worse?" he asked.

"Don't disappear, Jack. Don't hide."

"Molly…"

"Find some context, OK? Is this an opportunity?"

"I'm thinking there's not much of a market for sixty-five-year-old rock-and-pop critics."

"But we don't know, do we?"

Jack sighed. He sank deeper into pity.

She came over and kissed the top of his head. "I'm sorry, Jack. You deserve better."

"Did you have anything planned for tonight?"

She said, "Just us. At Table d'Hôte."

A small restaurant further north on the Upper East Side, close to where their first apartment had been. They'd had to scrimp and save and do everything short of gathering deposit bottles to afford it on their one-year anniversary. Back then, he wanted more than anything to be *The Observer*'s rock-and-pop critic. He had purpose and drive, the fire of youth. He saw a future as clearly as if it had already been written. To conceive is to achieve.

"I'll postpone," Molly offered.

"If it's all right, yeah. Good."

Jack pushed himself out of the chair with effort, as if the burden he felt was material rather than a weight on his psyche. "Time for a quick coffee?"

She looked at her smartphone. "I've got a three o'clock."

"Everybody's gone home in Africa. Europe, too."

"Not in Houston, though."

There was a dance festival in two weeks in Houston. He'd been told Björk was going to DJ. Maybe Molly could come along and do some business.

No, Jack realized. He wasn't going to Houston. He wasn't going to cover any festival from now on.

"Go to the movies, Jack. A museum. I'll get Suzi to call you."

"I might not answer," he replied, as he reached for the doorknob.

Jack walked the three-plus miles from Molly's office to Tribeca. Some part of him dropped away with each step: purpose, ambition, fulfillment, joy. No longer would he live in music. Vanquished, he was not welcomed where he had spent his best years.

His back aching, his knees too, he leaned against a hydrant by the African Burial Ground. The wind howled. Brian Wilson wrote of feeling like a leaf about to be blown away. So this is what he meant, thought Jack.

Jack had brought a Spalding rubber ball to the Wilson home. They played catch in his backyard, Brian and Melinda's dogs yipping louder and hopping higher with each toss.

Now he sighed. Freezing, he left the burial grounds and limped along Broadway. Soon, he was on Chambers Street, crowded with people hurrying for the subway. There was a queue on Broadway for a Staten Island-bound bus. Jack slithered between two taxis.

He entered his building and took the elevator alone to the eighth floor. He had no idea what he would find once he crossed the threshold of his apartment. Beyond the door was where he had done his work—in a tiny space, not much bigger than a closet, as comfortable as a pair of old boots. Desk, chair, Ex-Soft pencils in the cup, stack of red notebooks, Bob Marley bobblehead, beat-up old Gibson Hummingbird guitar perpetually out of tune.

In the filing cabinets were paper copies of every story he'd written for *The Observer*. Old vinyl on his shelves. On his corkboard were lists with the titles of forthcoming albums well into next year, of a proposed budget that would get him back to the U.K. Jarvis Cocker teased him, said he needed to upgrade his wardrobe. Said he would take Jack shopping next time he visited London. Johnny Marr told Jack to let him know when he returned to Manchester. They'd have dinner together.

His office was a museum piece now, a tribute to the long ago that was growing ever more distant by the heartbeat. A place where nothing new could be nurtured to life. Celebrate the recently deceased Jack. Churn it out while the body is still warm.

Go in there, Jack, and join the dead.

Days passed. Jack's misery remained.

Coming home after a long day at GSC, Molly said, "Jack, did you move from the sofa?"

Jack shrugged. He must have. A half-eaten tray of chocolate biscotti was on the ottoman.

"You're boycotting what exactly?" She was holding his desk calendar. Good ol' Jack still preferred pencil-and-paper. This band at 8:30 p.m., that band three hours later, five or six nights a week. "None of this ever again?"

He tied his robe as he stood. "What's the point in going to shows?"

"Enjoyment?" She stepped out of her heels. "I see you built your case against. But did you come up with any reasons in favor?"

"In favor of what?"

"Gee, I don't know…. Yourself?"

"Me? I don't exist."

"Ah. I love a cipher. Lucky me."

She proposed a Saturday brunch—a belated birthday celebration. Near the Seaport, Molly had the eggs benedict, Jack the crab cakes. A light rain coated the city.

"Happy birthday," Molly said, raising her Mimosa. "When do I get my Jack back?"

He apologized. "I'm no fun." He applied a wide smile. "Want me to fake it?"

"Cynicism is beneath you." A few minutes later: "I'm trying, Jack."

He looked at her. She was so lovely. Her eyes were the color of the Caribbean Sea. She hadn't aged a day.

"I'm just sorry to see you so…so defeated." She placed a sliver of Canadian bacon on his plate. "You're going to get over it. Have you thought about when?"

"It seems to be out of my control."

She shook her head. "You're not fighting back. That's my point."

Jack shrugged. The restaurant was spread out before him. It had been repurposed with a nautical theme, a nod to its role as a warehouse at the Fulton Fish Market, which had been erased from the neighborhood after it moved up to the Bronx.

Molly waited for his reply. She understood that Jack's commitment to his work masked a lifelong sense of alienation. In his way, he had found contentment, but there was more to him than he realized. Jack was thoughtful and kind and supportive and reliable and driven and tender, and he had no idea how cute he could be, that little pot belly, how he slid across the floor in his socks and brought her sample-sized bottles of shampoo from hotels and $10 bracelets he bought on Houston Street, and the way he looked at her when she called his name—a bit startled and curious, as if he was surprised that she was still there and in love with him.

But for all that, her Jack was the loneliest man she had ever known. Without something vital to occupy him and define him, she feared that Jack might fall apart. And then what?

There's only so much love can do.

"Don't let them make you a victim," she said now.

He responded with a sigh.

"All right then. How about we move on?" she said. "Even if we have to fake it for a while."

Define "a while," thought Jack, as he looked for the butter.

On Sunday, Molly took a flight to Amsterdam. Monday, Tuesday, whatever morning, Jack heard a dull buzz. He had no idea where he was. A wall of Marshalls were stacked behind a hidden door above the terrestrial sphere. An angel stamped the back of his hand, another angel brought him to the side of the stage. In the violet spotlight, David Bowie sang. He looked great: Tangerine hair spiked, makeup applied by Venus, he wore a gold lamé suit tailored by Yves Saint Laurent.

Jack sat up in bed and fumbled the phone from the nightstand. Through his fog, he saw it was Suzi. Muffled sunlight peaked past the blinds. It was almost 10 o'clock.

"Have you seen *Pitchfork* today?" she said.

"I'm not a fan." He cleared his throat. "Snarky. Besides, they hate me."

Pitchfork had a guy who monitored his Twitter feed and quoted his posts out of context. It was supposed to be some kind of slap against mainstream publications like *The Observer* and *the Times*, but it came across as cheap.

"They are reporting that you've been let go," Suzi said directly. "It's false. You have a new assignment."

"Somebody at *The Observer* leaked it?"

"I don't know, Jack."

He had snuggled into bed last night buoyed by intentions, however vague. But now reality was assaulting him and his feet hadn't touched the floor.

"Your conversations," he asked. "Were they contentious?"

"What conversations? You haven't sent me the package."

Puttering toward his office, he tried to picture Suzi. Petite, funky clothes always, primary colors, oversized plastic jewelry; sunbursty and ever energized. Molly said there was a trail of bodies of opposing lawyers who misread Susan Epstein-Lee and thought to step up cute.

"What is *Pitchfork*, Jack? Until Patti the Paralegal showed it to me, I had no idea it existed."

"It's a Condé Nast publication."

"*Vogue, Glamour*—that Condé Nast?"

Jack let out a groan. "Someone is trying to embarrass me."

"To what end?"

Jack shrugged. Surely, he had a rival somewhere at *The Observer*. He never could understand why someone liked him or didn't.

"Jack, we may have an opportunity here. Confidential information was revealed to media. Let me leverage this. You'll let it go, Jack, in exchange for the copyrights."

"I'm old fish."

"No. You are valued, in fact. They offered you a buyout. You have quite a few assignments. So, this blog is wrong. But Molly is right. You'll do your collection and everybody will be reminded of the good work you did. Opportunities may follow."

He was unconvinced.

"Why not come in this afternoon? A working lunch."

Jack hadn't shaved in days. He was still in his ratty PJ bottoms. "I'm in the middle of something," he said.

"All right. *Dis-moi*: Who is the contact in HR?"

He slipped the cover letter out of its manila envelope and read the name aloud. "You want the phone number?"

"Can you email me the documents?"

"I don't have a PDF. Just paper."

"Fax it. We'll pretend it's 1995."

"It's, like, twenty pages. Let me see if I can find a fax machine." There were about 14 Kinkos within walking distance.

On the wall above a box of old CDs was a framed photo of Bleecker Street he had taken on a winter's night back in 1970. He was a kid back then. Coming to Greenwich Village was an adventure, more so on that night, because subway service was erratic in the heavy snow. He had brought along his Instamatic, intending to document echoes of the magnetic vibe. When he looked west from LaGuardia Place, he saw Bleecker Street was all but empty. The lights on the Village Gate marquee were coated with thick snowflakes. Jack took out his little camera and, as a boxy yellow cab turned onto Bleecker, he clicked.

When he had the roll developed, he saw he had made a beautiful picture: the little sunbursts around the streetlights, the square-shouldered redbrick buildings, Bleecker Street as it disappeared toward Sixth Avenue, all in the gathering snow. And Jack had also captured something he hadn't seen: the strip of the Village where the clubs reigned was both inviting and foreboding, genial yet stern and eager to judge. Jack understood a musician would have to muster a lot of nerve to take it on.

"Jack?"

He had forgotten he was on the phone.

Signing off, he opened his mailbox. One hundred and nine emails. They were all variations of the same theme: "Is it true?" "Are you leaving *The Observer*?" And the less elegant: "Who's taking your place?"

"Thanks for getting in touch," he replied to all. "The story in *Pitchfork* is incorrect. Jack G. Rock and Pop Critic, *The New National Observer*."

He cced Lee Reinhard and bcced Suzi and Molly.

Among his remaining emails was one from a "demerson" with a Princeton.edu e-address. Likely not a publicist eager to pick at his corpse.

> *"Dear Mr. Fiorello,*
>
> *"I hope I haven't waited too long.*
>
> *"I understand you are retiring from your position at The New National Observer. I wanted to speak with you about my sister, the singer-songwriter Katy Shayne, who died tragically in Greenwich Village in 1977. I believe there is a story in Katy's life and death that is worthy of someone of your experience and reputation.*
>
> *"You may contact me at this address or by phone at your convenience. I will be quite glad to be of service.*
>
> *"Sincerely,*
>
> *Donald Emerson"*

Under his name was a phone number with a 609 area code and a 258 prefix.

Jack wrote back immediately. He thanked Emerson and said he would be in touch soonest—a word he typically used to mean "maybe never,"

He shut the laptop lid and sat in darkness.

Katy Shayne. Singer-songwriter.

He'd never heard of her.

A Friday night, and Jack had nowhere to be. He went to the window and stared down on Lower Broadway. Traffic was all but gone: a taxi, another taxi, a police car moving slowly; deliverymen on bicycles, plastic sacks in their baskets. Stragglers headed for the subways. The sky was dull and foreboding, but there was little wind. Molly would arrive safely and on time at JFK.

On the living room wall before him were two oversized canvas replicas of paintings by Paul Klee. "Tänzerin" was the portrait of a supple stick-figure woman dancing in a wash of golden yellows, violets, electric blues and pinks. Sharing the same color palette, "Fleeing Ghost" was open to interpretation, at least according to Molly. She believed the stick figure in "Fleeing Ghost" was dancing much as was the one in "Tänzerin." Disagreeing, Jack pointed to the stick figure's arm folded across her forehead, her other arm raised as if in defense. Her skirt and her legs told Jack she was running in fear.

He had a column to write but had no zeal for the task.

He told himself—actually, he repeated what Molly had said to him, and Suzi too. And maybe Charles Mingus during a conversation he had imagined just last night.

You are what you do, Jack.

If you do nothing…

He put on a button-down shirt and fresh jeans.

He had been staring at *The Rockford Files* on TV—Dan Ferguson played the guitar solos in *The Rockford Files* and *Barney Miller* themes—when he heard the squeak of luggage wheels. When Molly entered the apartment, he stood to greet her.

She let out a sigh of relief.

"Welcome home," he said.

Jack got a hug and a long kiss on the lips.

"Tired?" he asked.

"A bit dazed, I think." She began to unbutton her suit jacket. "Did you hear from Suzi?"

"I did." He hadn't returned her call.

Molly was in the bedroom now. "Did she tell you we're seeing them tomorrow night? Suzi and Henry?"

"Why?"

"What 'why'?"

"Why are we doing that? Seeing them?"

Molly stood in her bra and panties, black against her smooth and ageless skin. "I thought we'd get out on a Saturday night."

"With Suzi? This doesn't sound like a good idea."

"Anyone else will ask you about music, *The Observer*, celebrities. With Suzi and Henry, we'll have drinks and dinner."

"Why not just us?"

"Could we have fun?" she asked. "I need a buffer if you get melancholy."

Jack couldn't disagree.

Molly debated whether to hang up the suit or set it aside for the cleaners. "We haven't been out on a Saturday night—no music, just out—in how long? Ages."

"Ages," he agreed.

Molly removed her bra and went to the drawer for fresh pajamas.

"I'm not insensitive," she said. "You deserve better. You're so good."

She put on the cotton top and began to do up the buttons. Then she stopped. She looked at Jack.

She removed her top and, stepping toward him, kissed his lips softly, and then again, her hand clasping the back of his neck.

"You and me, Jack. This can't change. Not ever."

"No, of course not," he said as he stirred. "Never."

"I'll get us some wine."

He began to undress.

Chapter Three

Getting ready for their night out, Molly mentioned the first time she and Jack had spent an evening with Suzi and her husband, Henry, reminding him that he had been prickly.

"So don't jump all over him if he mentions the Steely Dans," she said, crossing the bedroom, inserting a yellow pearl earring.

"He won't," Jack replied as he buttoned his shirt.

"They're on your side."

Back then, Suzi and Henry, an executive at Pfizer who oversaw charitable giving, were hosting a cocktail party in their perfectly appointed four-bedroom on Sutton Place that overlooked the East River. As a teen in Tennessee, Henry had gone to Northwest Prep Academy, then headed to Vanderbilt where he majored in Pharmacology before earning an MBA. From across the room, Jack could see he was very comfortable in his own skin. He kept the conversation moving among the corporate types who surrounded him.

With Molly networking, Jack had been abandoned. He would have preferred to be in a sweat-soaked club, a band frying his face, but he was dutiful—not a chore; he loved the hell out of Molly and would've kneeled on rice if she asked. As the party rolled on, he found himself elbow-to-elbow with the affable host.

"Are we taking good care of you?" Henry asked. The gray in his blond hair shone under track lighting. In his early-to-mid 40s he was taller than Jack, with a swimmer's coiled athleticism. "Suzi said you've spent your entire career at *The Observer*."

"I have. But I don't know a stock from a bond."

"No, I know your work. Music. Impressive. A cherry on top."

Jack nodded in gratitude. "So, you went to prep school in Memphis, college in Nashville. Who were you listening to when you were coming up?"

Henry Lee said, "Steely Dan."

"Well, that explains the lounge music." Jack pointed to the air, now soiled by smooth jazz.

Henry seemed puzzled. "I thought you folks were over the moon for the Dan."

"You had B.B. King and Bobby Blue Bland and Al Green on one side of you, and the Ryman and the Opry on the other, and you picked Steely Dan?"

"I—"

"Steely Dan is decaf Frappuccino, man. It's self-impressed hipster bullshit for people who think of music as validation. Next thing you know, you'll be telling people your IQ. You're better than that."

Henry seemed dazed.

"What's your favorite album?" Jack asked.

"By Steely Dan? 'Aja,' I would say."

"Who's Wayne Shorter?"

"I don't—"

"Adding a second to a triad doesn't make you Horace Silver. It's like claiming you speak Italian because you can say, I don't know, 'Frappuccino.'"

"Well, you're the expert, but—"

"What's your streaming service?" Jack asked. "I'm going to make you a playlist that will knock you loopy. Seriously. I'm locking you in the Blue Note vault until you come out a champion. Molly says you're excellent, so I'm gonna do that."

Now, on the trip down to Broadway, Jack and Molly had the elevator to themselves, though the scent of someone else's Chinese delivery lingered.

"God, I was such a dick," he said, remembering.

"Were you?"

"I believe you said 'petulant.'"

He looked at their reflection on the elevator door. Under a khaki topcoat, he wore that shirt Molly always liked, a black blazer, black jeans and his gray boots. As a contrary response to Suzi's rainbow colors, Molly chose a muted rust jacket, black top and slacks, and a necklace Jack had picked up in Monterey, hippie stars and half-moons. Jack thought they looked like adults.

The elevator jerked as they landed in the lobby. A cab pulled up as if it had been summoned.

Henry Lee, in a blue double-breasted blazer and gray slacks, hugged Jack.

Peck-peck went Suzi, and they were swept into the living room, Jack's coat now in Henry's arms.

Suzi wore a twinkly red dress above her knees, a yellow plastic belt, a necklace of yellow plastic triangles that matched her earrings, and red-and-yellow lacquered heels.

"Ah," Jack said, pointing to the music in the air.

Henry nodded with pride. He was spinning a British singer/spoken-word artist who deployed his rumbling bass voice over slinky electronic rock: son of Massive Attack.

"I didn't know they made music like this," Henry said.

Suzi said, "Henry researched your 'best of' lists for the past five years. He's been buying CDs."

"Propping up the industry," Jack said.

"What are you drinking?" Henry asked.

"Your call."

Molly volunteered to help Henry retrieve the hors d'oeuvres.

Suzi pointed Jack toward a floral sofa.

"That didn't take long," he said. "Feels orchestrated. Not improvised."

"They're giving us a chance to talk," Suzi replied.

They sat with their backs to the East Side skyline.

"I dig the new eyeglasses," Jack said. "Not so...severe."

"How are you?"

He replied, "I'm surprising myself. You two?"

"We're fine. Henry, you know... He's a rock."

"I like that guy," he said. "Did you tell him about *The Observer*?"

She shrugged sheepishly.

"Is attorney-client privilege really a thing?"

"With Henry, I work around it."

"No worries. I tell Molly everything," he said. "Adulterers, thieves. Men who don't wash their hands in the bathroom."

She said, "We just want to be certain you're all right."

"I'm figuring it out. Really."

"Hold tight," she advised. "Legal might resist, but when they kick it to Editorial, you'll get what you want."

"Oh, I doubt it..."

Molly returned with a silver tray of salmon and dark rye bread. Capers and chopped onion.

At the restaurant, Molly, Suzi and Henry drifted into work-speak before the *boquerones* arrived: patient advocacy, disease awareness, a wastewater treatment facility in Cameroon, a seminar on HIV/AIDS sponsored by the Open Society Foundations. Now and then, Jack listened. He was no more essential to the conversation than the napkin on his lap. Saying nothing, he went elsewhere: Tom Waits at the Orpheum Theatre in Phoenix, Maceo Parker at the Roxy in L.A., Anna Calvi at London's Hammersmith Odeon.

And then: Katy Shayne. Singer-songwriter.

Who?

No, he hadn't heard of her.

But he should have. Per her brother, she was a musician who died tragically in 1977. In the Village. That was the kind of thing young Jack was unlikely to miss.

Unless she was so obscure that the death didn't register as news.

"Singer-songwriter" suggested a professional or at least someone who wasn't just knocking around. Someone with a goal.

Was her death related in any way to her career?

In his email, Emerson suggested as much: "I believe there is a story in Katy's life and death that is worthy of someone of your experience and reputation."

Meaning someone who could understand where she fit in.

Did she fit in?

"Jack."

Henry? Ah, the restaurant. Dinner for four.

"Sorry."

Katy Shayne, he thought. How did I miss it?

Back at his desk, Jack opened his *Observer* email account. During the weekend, he had accumulated 318 messages from publicists, mostly blast emails, this new album, that new track, a tour lined up. He scanned quickly. Amid the typhoon of pitches and flackery was a note from the assistant editor who handled his copy. There were minimal edits on his latest piece. She always improved his stories. They had never quarreled.

Before Jack wrote his reply, he realized it would soon be the final time they would work together on a Jack G. story about a living musician.

"All good," Jack typed. "Thanks much." He clicked "send."

"Done," said Jack to no one.

Showered, shaved: It's what productive people do. He put on his scarf and leather coat and, red notebook in his pocket, headed out. He settled on an old boxcar-style diner, young moms lingering over brunch, a workingman's crowd gathering as the lunch hour approached. Jack took a booth in the back corner and watched the yellow taxis fly by until the silver-haired waitress arrived and then he ordered a burger and curly fries.

He took out his phone, checked his contacts list and called a publicist at BMI, a performance-rights organization that collected licensing fees on recordings and live sets for its member composers and publishers. He identified himself as Jack Fiorello, *The New National Observer*. The paper's name earned immediate attention.

"I'm trying to track down a composer. Katy Shayne," he said. "She died in 1977. Do you have any information?"

"Hold on," the publicist replied. Click-click on the keyboard. "Someone pays her annual membership fee."

"Really?" Jack asked. "I couldn't find any evidence of her recordings. She's not on Spotify or Apple Music. Nothing on YouTube."

Jack could tell she was scanning a database.

"She registered nine songs with us in…1971 and '72."

"Would you email me the titles?"

Jack's burger had arrived. The busy waitress smiled curtly and hurried off on white rubber soles.

"Also, who is paying her dues?"

"I'm not sure I can tell you that. But I can write and tell him you'd like to speak to him."

"Is it a Donald Emerson?"

Her hesitation told him it was. He slapped at the ketchup bottle. "Nine songs, huh? Any action?"

"No," she said.

"Ever?"

"Never."

"Yet her brother still pays her dues."

Herm Odell was a pain in the ass when Jack first met him and—there was universal agreement on this—remained a pain in the ass in the decades since. Gruff, scruffy and now given to wearing his pants high over his inner-tube belly, Odell received scant mention in the chronicles of the Greenwich Village folk era—as if to define him, historians liked to point out that there was no Odell's West, even though he had claimed it was San Francisco's best music venue. "They Started at Odell's" read the sign in the window as had ads in the now defunct *Village Voice*. Technically, it was true. If they could sing in the neighborhood of pitch and strum the guitar without dropping it, they had—and then moved up to the second-worst club. The walls of his charmless joint, which was long and narrow like a railroad flat, were lined with faded publicity stills of Judy Collins, Freddie Neil, Buffy Sainte-Marie and countless others, their Herm Odell-praising salutations and signatures all in the same hand.

With hyperbole, outright lies and the rights of ownership of the Bleecker Street building in which it sat, Odell kept his club alive and ran an open-mike night three or four times a week. He paid the musicians nothing; he charged them for drinks. But young, eager and impressionable, they didn't seem to mind because he entertained them with stories that made them feel they were one or two degrees of separation from superstardom. He told them Dave Van Ronk might have been the Mayor of MacDougal Street, but Herm Odell was the King of Greenwich Village. "If you're here the next time Bob drops in, you can ask him," Odell told them, omitting that Dylan never dropped in. Dylan hadn't spoken to Odell since about 1961, when they fought over a cab.

But for all his self-consumed bluster, his prodigious memory proved somewhat dependable: If you removed him from the tales he told, they were in proximity to what had actually happened. He was a prime starting point for any story that connected to music made in the Village.

Unzipping his coat, Jack held onto the rail as he descended toward the stench of stale beer. Eyes adjusting to the darkness, he saw on the stage a burly, bearded man in his early 20s playing Piedmont blues for an audience of no one. Working a Furry Lewis number via Bromberg and Kaukonen, the young man wasn't bad, but he had chosen a tricky style that required a dexterity he hadn't yet developed and was struggling his way through. Jack admired his commitment, but that was never enough: No one who came to play the Village wasn't committed.

Jack turned to the bartender who, oblivious to the music, was counting out greenbacks, separating singles, fives and 10s into little piles. She wore a puffy coat against the cold. Odell was a skinflint landlord, even if he punished himself by turning down the steam heat.

"Is Herm in back?" he asked.

Without looking up, she nodded.

"Better give me a beer."

He put down a 10 for a dripping long neck.

Jack waited until the song ended. As he walked through the silence, he caught the musician's eye and nodded respectfully.

Jack knocked on the frame of the office door and let himself in. Odell was behind the desk, surrounded by mountains of paperwork. He had a metal shield over an eye that Jack assumed had been the subject of recent surgery. A cigarette clung to his bottom lip. He wore a navy topcoat.

"Jack Fiorello," he said, pointing with a nicotine-stained finger. *"The*

Observer."

"How are you, Herm?"

The young bluesman's next number crackled through a speaker high in the corner.

"What about this kid?" Odell asked.

"Hire him."

"I had Blind Blake, you know."

Blind Blake died in the 1930s.

"Blind Boy Fuller."

Dead in the '40s. Jack said, "You mean Reverend Gary Davis?"

"Ingrate." Odell rubbed his chin and throat with vigor as if to shake off the cold. "What do you want, Jack?"

"I'm working on a thing," he said, putting the beer bottle on the desk. "A folk singer who died suddenly in the 1970s."

"Phil Ochs. That rally in Central Park? 'The War is Over' with Belafonte, Seeger, Joan Baez? My idea. So, who's crying now?"

Shaking his head, Jack said, "This was a woman. Died. Killed. Maybe an act of violence?"

"You're thinking I'm going to remember some dame who died fifty-something years ago."

Dame? "If not you, who?" Jack said.

Odell liked that. "Drugs?"

"I don't know, Herm."

He groped for an ashtray. "Give me her name."

"Katy Shayne."

"She killed herself?"

Jack hesitated. "Did she?"

Odell said, "A girl singer. Folk. Good songs. Good voice." Moaning, he hoisted his body out of his chair. "Cute, but not a stunner. Shy."

"Katy Shayne," Jack repeated. "I'm not placing her, Herm. Did she record?"

"Maybe," Odell replied as he jiggled around the desk.

Jack followed as the club owner thudded by. On stage, the bearded bluesman had finished his song and was waiting for a reaction. Jack watched as Odell waved him over: sit, negotiate. Don't pay to play, Jack thought to say as the young man looped his guitar strap over his hat.

"Herm, she's mediocre, but you remember her?"

Odell turned. "Did I say she was mediocre?"

"'Good voice.' 'Cute.' Faint praise."

"I also said 'good songs.' The kid could write a song. That I remember."

In his red notebook, Jack scribbled: Katy Shayne could write a song.

"Back then, Jack, somebody cute and shy is going to break through? The competitors were warriors. Hurricanes. You forget I was there when Janis nearly gutted that son of a bitch—"

"Katy Shayne," Jack interrupted. "Where was she from? Do you know?"

"You write, but do you quote me? Appreciate me?"

"You gave me a name, Herm. I appreciate it. But you know I can't make promises."

Best I can do, he thought, is pitch you as a subject for an In Memoriam.

"One more," Jack said. "How did she die?"

"13th Street off Fifth," Odell said as he reached for a chair. "Off the roof." With characteristic subtlety, he made a gesture indicating a high dive that landed with a crash.

Jack grimaced. "Jesus."

"Yeah. A career move if you used to have a career," Odell said. The chair groaned and wobbled as he settled in. Jack tapped him on the shoulder with his notebook, said "thanks again" and sat on the lukewarm radiator near the bar. Using the web browser on his phone, he searched for information on Katy Shayne. Finding none, he looked under her legal name, Emerson, adding Katy, then Kate, then Katherine. And there it was: The *Daily News* called it a fall, but also said, awkwardly, that suicide hasn't been ruled out. Two grafs in total. No mention of her music.

Zipping up his coat, slinging his scarf around his neck, he exited at Bleecker Street accompanied by a familiar stirring. Something was awry; things weren't adding up. He trusted the instinct.

A half-hour or so later, Jack arrived at Fifth and 13th, having passed through

Washington Square Park, populated as always with students, neighborhood seniors, nannies with strollers, skateboarders, tourists and musicians, all with a high tolerance for the cold. He turned east at an upscale boutique on the ground floor of a condo where once stood the Lone Star Café, New York's citadel of country music in the '70s and '80s. There was no marker to indicate that Johnny and June, George and Tammy, Waylon and Jessi, or any other members of country royalty had played right here back then.

Much of 13th Street had changed as if to match the New School University Center's recently completed tower with its glass walls, exposed staircases and brass skin. Industrial-chic restaurants and a showroom for an interior design firm stood where once were bodegas, newsstands and photocopy shops. But by mid-block, Jack saw the remnants of the 13th Street he knew. Above the barren trees were red-brick buildings with Art Deco touches, iron-work balconies and fire escapes, and wooden water tanks set against a sullen sky. On the south side was a tall, white Beaux Arts building better suited to Tribeca with its balustrades and granite columns.

Jack looked up to the cornice and he let his eyes follow the building past its arches all the way down to the sidewalk.

Chapter Four

A three-pee night. Jesus. Septuagenarian rockers still toured—Willie Nelson still toured, and he's 85—but none wrote about their shrinking bladders. After his third visit to the bathroom, he looked through the darkness at Molly, who had curled herself into a ball. Jack toggled the quilt comforter until she was covered.

He went into his office, opened his laptop and responded to Donald Emerson's email:

When can we talk? He gave him his number.

Less than a minute after he hit send, an instant message buzzed his phone.

"Insomnia too? This is Don Emerson."

Jack wrote, "Call in the morning?"

Emerson replied, "You're in NYC? Come down to Princeton. I have things you might want to see."

"Could be," Jack wrote. "When?"

"Whenever?"

"Will be in touch. Good night."

Coming in from a pitch meeting at the Battery, Molly caught Jack at work, his material spread across the sofa and ottoman. He employed actual, not virtual, file folders. He printed articles onto paper. Used a stapler, yellow markers, multi-colored sticky notes. Somewhere in his desk, he kept a tiny jar of Wite-Out.

"You look…better," she said, as she put down her tote. "Are you yourself?"

"I've more or less blasted through the stages of grief."

Pointing to his mess, she said, "Is this about the singer-songwriter you never heard of? I'm impressed."

"Hold off," he said. "Could just be busy work."

Three days later, Jack caught a mid-morning train out of Penn Station. He sat solo in a seat for two and, sipping cardboard coffee, reviewed his notes as the trip south began underground.

He found no evidence that Katy Shayne had much of a career prior to her death. He compiled a list of clubs on or near Bleecker Street in the early '70s that featured several singer-songwriters per night: the Bitter End, Café Au Go Go, Café Wha? the Gaslight, Gerdes Folk City, the Kettle of Fish, Odell's East, the Night Owl and on and on. Combing through ancient ads in *the Voice*, he saw the names of scores of artists who had made some sort of mark and many, many, many more who vanished without tribute. Searching until his eyes blurred, he didn't see Katy Shayne in any ad or review. That didn't mean she didn't appear in the clubs—Odell indicated she knocked around the circuit—but it suggested the owners didn't see her as a draw. No critic who wrote for *the Voice* or *the Times* covered one of her sets.

Despite that, Katy registered her compositions with the Library of Congress. She signed with BMI. She had expected success.

As the New Jersey Transit train rattled into sunlight, Jack opened his notebook and reviewed the Katy Shayne song titles BMI had sent him. He was trying to suss out a theme.

"Camera"

"Secrets of a Shy Girl"

"Celia Remains"

"That Didn't Last Too Long"

"A Lover's Prayer"

"(I Dreamed of) Audrey Munson"

"She's Got the Look"

"Gillian Holroyd"

"Last Chance to Wave Goodbye"

They weren't alphabetized, so Jack assumed they were presented in the order in which they were registered. Could be Katy wrote "Camera" first, then "Secrets of a Shy Girl" and so on. As the train chugged along and his coffee swam in its paper cup, he noticed a shift in tone about halfway through the list. Without hearing the lyrics, top line or chord structure, Jack could only guess, but the first two titles seemed confessional and thus autobiographical—not an unusual approach for an emerging singer-songwriter. He didn't know what to make of "A Lover's Prayer," but two of the next four songs might've indicated growth by embracing a new narrative technique: She could work out issues by identifying with the plight of the song's name-sake stand-ins.

Jack knew something about Audrey Munson. In the early part of the 20th century, she was the model, often nude, for at least a dozen statues in New York City. From the always-temporary height of fame, she had a terrible, tragic downfall, resulting in a suicide attempt by poison. Her star extinguished, Audrey Munson was committed by her mother to a psychiatric institution, where she lived for 65 years until she died at age 104. Jack wondered if Katy Shayne had portrayed Munson in bold triumph or broken beyond hope.

"Gillian Holroyd" was a name Jack didn't recognize. It sounded to him like the handle of a British folk singer, maybe a lesser-known among the musicians who played the London circuit in the early 1960s. He searched in Wiki as the train eased into a station to discharge passengers a few stops before his destination. No one gave a second glance to the man with the red notebook as he focused on his tiny screen.

Gillian Holroyd was the name of the character played by Kim Novak in "Bell, Book and Candle," a film released in 1958. As the train lurched ahead, Jack recalled that Novak played a witch who lived in Greenwich Village. She ran around barefoot, had a Siamese cat and was nothing like a shy girl.

Katy Shayne: a girl wary of fame or a free spirit eager to soar in the Village?

Soon, the train arrived in Princeton and Jack exited, stepping gingerly. He found the air clear, chilled, pleasant.

Don Emerson stood at the edge of the parking lot, scoping the passengers with hesitant anticipation. He waved at the man with the red notebook.

Tall but slightly hunched, his face long and narrow, Emerson wore a houndstooth cap, a brown knee-length wool coat and forest-green corduroy slacks. Jack saw a tie and a white shirt beneath his scarf. Emerson's duck boots were untied, as if he had slipped them on after kicking off his office shoes.

They shook hands.

"Do I look like her? People say I do, but I don't know..."

"I've never seen her," Jack replied. "I'm just starting out."

"I've got photos."

A pale grey-green Prius was waiting. With the click of a fob, Emerson opened its door and Jack eased onto the passenger's side. When Emerson settled behind the wheel, he removed his cap to reveal his hair up top was reduced to a few strands. His head brushed the ceiling.

"Any preference? For where you want to start. Any particular, you know, place?"

"Wherever you think tells the story," Jack said as he unzipped his leather coat.

"We grew up not far from here. In Hopewell. Hopewell, New Jersey. There are many Hopewells. You probably know that. But, no, it was Hopewell, New Jersey."

He's nervous, Jack thought. Uncertain and a bit timid. He wants it to go well and worries it might not.

"Do you want to see the house? Not that it's still ours. No, I don't...not anymore. My dad sold it before Katy died."

"Why?" Jack asked as they left the lot.

"See the house? I thought, you know, start at the beginning?"

"No, I meant, why did your dad sell it."

Emerson shrugged. "I think, after my mother died, family life wasn't of interest. He knew Katy wasn't coming back once she got to New York. No chance of that."

Jack made a note. "What do you do?"

"I work in student finance at Princeton. Been there my whole career. Yep. The Office of Finance & Treasury. Like a bursar."

"What's a bursar?"

"We manage student accounts. Tuition."

"I always thought it would be cool to work at a college." At least once a year, Jack covered a concert held at a campus auditorium, arriving early and soaking up in the environment. "The kids. Lots of energy. The last roundup before the clampdown."

"I enjoy it. Like I said, I've been there, what, about forty years."

They entered a roundabout and headed up a tree-lined hill. A light coating of snow-topped prickly bushes that ringed a brick building.

"Thinking about retiring?" Jack asked.

"And do what?"

"I don't know." Jack nodded toward the miniature stuffed tiger that hung from the rearview mirror. "Play with the grandkids?"

"Oh, my wife put that there. We don't have kids. Or grand…my wife. Betty. Elizabeth, actually. She's playful. Like Katy was." He chuckled. "People thought my sister was shy. We're—no, Katy wasn't shy. She held back. She was cautious. Reserved. When she was young, I think, given her nature, it was… She was hurt too easily. People would say things. Exclude her. It wasn't easy for her."

"Why not, Don?"

They slowed to a halt at a Stop sign. "Our mother died suddenly. Hit by a car. There, gone. My father, he was the kind of man…he didn't give a you-know-what."

As they proceeded up the hill, Emerson turned. "So, yes, in that way, Katy and I, we were alike. Reserved. But I always said New York gave Katy the tough hide she needed."

"The music business will do that," Jack said.

The Prius hummed through an intersection and onto the parking lot of a self-storage facility. Emerson had told Jack whatever he had of Katy's, save a few photos he kept at home, were held here, the latest in a series of facilities he had rented after his father sold the family house.

As they drove along, he said, "I suppose I always had it in my mind that Katy's story hadn't been told. You know? That she died, and so her songs died, and that's that. And that bothered me. Of course, when I thought of her, I missed my sister and imagined the kind of good life she could've had. But every now and then, I'd think, 'Her music? It's not dead. It's stored away. It's just, you know, *unheard*.'"

"So why now, Don? Years have passed. Decades."

"Well, I'm not getting any younger. When I heard you were retiring, I thought, 'Maybe there aren't too many music writers who were around in the Seventies.'"

"You heard I had retired?"

"One of the interns said. She knew I read *The Observer*. I'd photocopy your stories about folk singers. The upcoming songwriters. Women in the business."

They exited the Prius, entered the building and took the elevator to the third floor. Emerson carried a handwritten note: 36th row, locker 17.

Flooded with sunlight through the building's glass façade, the storage facility was spotless: institutional gray-green rug and beige lockers of various sizes, some as high as the ceiling. On their way to the 36th row, they passed dollies and rolling aluminum staircases.

"Seems impersonal," Emerson said, "but it's…once you get in there, you feel it's your own. Private, at least."

"No, I know." Jack and Molly had a space in a storage unit on Vesey Street in Manhattan, around the corner from City Winery, where, indulging his delight in quality, Jack dropped in on Los Lobos every time they were in town.

Emerson found row 36 and then located locker 17. It was about the size of a generous closet in most Manhattan apartments, well short of roomy. Nothing taller than a household ladder would fit inside.

Emerson produced a key.

The door swung open. There were two boxes on the floor; one large, maybe five feet square, the other the 18-inch size. Yellowed tape secured both boxes. A guitar case leaned against the pale back wall.

"That's it?" Quickly, Jack added, "Sorry."

Emerson stepped back. "I guess it is kind of, I don't know, pathetic."

"How do you want to do this?"

He shrugged.

"I can just sit on the floor…"

Jack took off his coat and, ducking down, stepped into the locker. He sat cross-legged next to the smaller box. Coat and notebook on the carpet, he took out his pen.

"OK?"

Arms folded, Emerson nodded. "It's been a while…"

Using the ballpoint, Jack slit the tape on the smaller box and yanked back its flaps.

High-school memorabilia. A faded diploma, yearbook, citations and ribbons, report cards, a trophy for swim team. The scent of moth balls, of a childhood long passed.

Jack reached in and pulled out a well-worn spiral-ring notebook. On the cover, in the florid script, was written: "Katherine Shayne." The signature was surrounded by flowers, daisies mostly, and puffy clouds.

"Why Shayne?" Jack asked.

"She was planning her stage name. It kind of rolls off the tongue."

Jack thumbed through the lined pages. It was a diary of sorts and a collection of fragments of ideas. Some doodles, poems, quotations from lyrics.

"Look at this," Jack said, holding an open page up to Emerson. "Looks like she started a song, then let it go."

"I think I remember that."

"Heck of a title. 'Every Little Bit Hurts.'" Jack read aloud. "Every little bit hurts / Every word they say / What they think of me / And why I must obey." She had made simple chord notations. It opened on a G chord; the second line went to a D, then to F#7 for the next two lines. Pretty clever, Jack thought. Ominous. Goodbye, daisies and puffy clouds.

"Mind if I take this?" he asked.

Emerson said no, not at all. "That's why we're here."

Putting down the notebook, he reached into the box and pulled out a handful of cassettes, their plastic cases held together with a rubber band.

"Maybe she recorded that one," Jack mused. "I'd like to see where it went."

"She had, Katy, a cassette recorder in her bedroom. Nothing, you know, professional, but she bought a real microphone. It's in the box. It should be."

It was.

"I'd like to borrow these tapes," Jack said. "I can get them cleaned up and copied. Convert them to files."

"Please. Whatever." Emerson smiled. "I wonder what Katy would make of this. Jack from *The Observer* listening to her childhood tapes. She'd probably be embarrassed. Or not. I don't know."

"Everybody starts somewhere." Jack inched toward the hard-shell guitar case. He unsnapped the latches. He found inside a big-bodied Guild D-40 in natural wood. There was an old-fashioned pickup across the sound hole. Of course, it wasn't old-fashioned four decades ago.

"When's the last time someone played this?" Jack asked.

"Probably the last time Katy did," Emerson replied. "I don't. Betty doesn't play either."

Jack took out the guitar and sat it on his lap. He could smell the wood as well as the dust. "Do you know when she got this?"

"My mom bought it for her. I'd say 1968? I'm guessing... She worked at the Chocolate Factory. Hopewell Dainties. Remember those?"

Jack pointed at the guitar. "This Guild wasn't cheap. Might have cost eight hundred dollars or something like that. For a working woman in 1968, that's a commitment."

"My mom drove me and Katy to the factory in Hoboken. She let Katy pick it out. Katy would have been, let's see, fifteen? But Mom knew Katy was serious. Katy was like that. Once she got a thought in her head, man, look out." He let out a little laugh. "Determined? If I had her willpower—"

"You loved her," Jack observed as he returned the guitar to its case.

"She was my big sister. I thought...well, I was certain Katy hung the moon."

Guitar back in its corner, Jack retrieved the yearbook. He flipped through the pages until he found the senior portraits. Then he located Katy.

She had long black hair, dark eyes, a narrow face, full lips, rounded chin with a hint of a dimple. A pretty teen. She wore hoop earrings and a peasant top with a scoop neck and embroidered flowers.

"A good likeness?" Jack asked, turning the book toward Emerson.

He nodded.

"She's not smiling…"

"She counted the hours until she could leave for Greenwich Village. My mother insisted she finish school. She did, barely. The nest couldn't hold her. Not Katy."

"Purposeful," Jack said. "A purposeful hippie."

"That's about it."

"Says here she was in Band, Glee Club and the Mathematics Club. The Math Club?"

"My mother again. Something to fall back on. Not that Katy was going to, you know, fall back. Like I said, she was determined."

Jack put the yearbook next to his coat and the stack of cassettes. "Good for her. No one makes it by luck, no matter what you hear."

But in less than a decade, she kills herself, Jack thought as he reached toward the big box.

"You won't like what's in that one," Emerson said with a grimace.

Chapter Five

A paper bag with the same texture as a brown, grocery-store carryall but twice its size, property of the New York City Police Department. An NYPD shield under the lettering. On the back, a line and on it numbers applied with a rubber stamp: 06/01/77. An illegible signature on the next line, faded almost to invisible.

"The day after she died," Emerson said. "She died on May 31."

Jack put the sack on his lap. "What was the protocol? Her personal effects stay with the body until the coroner releases it? If it's a suicide, is it evidence? Evidence of what?"

"Open it, Jack. It's all right."

With Emerson trailing, Jack walked the bag out of the locker and found a table against a glass wall. Tipping the bag, he slid out its contents.

"Ah, Christ," he muttered.

Pink blood-stained panties and a thin necklace had tumbled out first.

Jack felt around inside the bag with the tip of his pen. Out dropped a pink bra, lace with underwiring. It was also coated in dried blood.

"There's something…" he said. "It's stuck."

He put down the pen and reached in with his bare fingers.

A sling bag, its festive Indian colors muted by time.

Jack offered it to Don, who declined.

He placed it next to the bloody garments and the necklace.

Now, Jack looked into the paper bag. He lifted it, turned it over, shook it. Nothing came out but a musty scent.

"That's it," he said.

A fall from atop a tall building. Blood and viscera. Her clothes had to be discarded.

Emerson had picked up the necklace and its heart-shaped pendant. "Mom gave this to her," he said softly as he let it hang from his fingers.

Jack put the bra and panties back in the NYPD sack. Then, reaching for the sling bag, he asked, "Do you remember what's inside?"

"A roach clip," said Emerson with a sheepish grin. "Rolling papers."

"Signs of the times."

Jack shook the bag. Big Bambu rolling papers fell out. So did a forceps-style roach clip. A ChapStick. A retractable four-ink BIC pen. An unopened pack of stick gum: Wrigley's Spearmint.

"I'm just a music critic," Jack said, "but I'd ask who buys a pack of gum before killing themselves?"

A change purse, an elastic capo, a book of matches.

"From the Lone Star," he said, examining the matches. "Did she play there?"

Emerson said he didn't know.

"Big place for country music. It went out of business in '89." He looked at Emerson. "It was down the block from where she died."

As Jack took up the change purse, Emerson said, "I know what you're going to find. Five dollars and seventy-nine cents in coins. Four subway tokens. And her driver's license. Meager."

Emerson was right. It was all the currency his sister had on her the night she died. As for the license, she looked dour, an expression the photographers at the Motor Vehicle Department can generate as well as capture. "She was living on Charles Street, I see."

"At Marta's. Yes."

"Marta?"

"You should talk to her." Emerson was checking the time on his phone.

"Do you have to run?"

"I'd better get back. I should."

In the bottom of the sling back, Jack found a pair of turquoise earrings whose wires had caught on the dyed cotton, a couple of picks, and a red coaster from the Lone Star Café—the "Best Honky Tonk North of Abilene."

When Jack turned it over, he saw a phone number with a 615 area code.

"That's Nashville," said Jack as he began to repack the change purse and sling bag. "Katy ever go to Nashville?"

Emerson said, "Yes, she did. Moved there in late '75, I think. Maybe early '76."

As Jack put the coaster in his notebook, he glanced at the necklace and its heart-shaped pendant on the table.

"Take whatever you need," Emerson said, as he repacked the NYPD sack. "The necklace, too. Otherwise, it'll just be locked away again."

They headed back past silent homes and barren trees. Jack sat with his knees together, holding the yearbook, Katy's notebook, and her cassettes on his thighs. In his coat pocket with his red Moleskine was her necklace and earrings, one of her picks, and the matchbook and coaster from the Lone Star. For no reason other than he wanted one, he also took an old New York City subway token, the kind he hadn't seen in decades.

He thanked Emerson as they passed through the outskirts of the Princeton campus, students hurried between Gothic buildings against the cold. "I don't know what I expected, but it wasn't all this."

"If it helps, I'm glad. I wanted to do this for years. Like I said, her story, her music—does it end just like that? No one knows, no one hears? You know, I get it. I do. Her career wasn't going like she dreamed and she breaks, but—"

"She was depressed?"

"Not clinically, I suppose. Or maybe. I don't..." He looked both ways and then entered the intersection. The train station was in view. "I hadn't spoken to her in a while. I didn't know she was back from Nashville. But since she was a child, she wanted to write songs and sing them. And it wasn't working out, was it? She put in years—her whole life, really—and nothing happened for her."

"Well, 'nothing' may be overstating it."

"Given all that she had been through, I guess I wasn't totally surprised. After the shock, I mean. After the sick feeling that I would never see my sister again."

They bounced into the parking lot. Jack had no idea when the train back to New York would arrive, but he wanted to find a quiet spot to memorialize Emerson's asides.

"You said 'All she'd been through.' Was it more than it wasn't happening like she wanted it to? Bad manager or something. A deal gone sour?"

The Prius glided into a spot near the stone station house. "I don't know if she had a manager. But I think it was mounting pressure. I mean, it wasn't easy to be gay and out back then."

"Wait—Katy was gay?"

"Gay and out." He shook his head. "Wasn't easy in Hopewell either. Or with my father."

Jack thought of Katy's teenage lyric: "Every little bit hurts / Every word they say / What they think of me / And why I must obey." The pressure to conform in the face of rejection, of prejudice and misunderstanding. She was under its heel as a young teen at home and at school.

They both heard the harsh bleat of a train horn in the near distance. Jack gathered Katy's material.

Emerson apologized for having to rush back to the office. "Talk to Marta," he told Jack as they shook hands. "Marta Pacheco. She's a lawyer. Betty and I get a Christmas card from her every year. I can email you her address."

As the northbound train wheezed into the station, Jack thanked Emerson again. Arms full, he left the warmth of the car.

Back in his kitchen, Jack parboiled and then crushed plum tomatoes and tossed them into the garlic and olive oil in the frying pan. As they hissed and sputtered, he added red pepper flakes and then stirred in the biggest basil leaves. He augmented the fresh tomatoes with canned puree, not too much.

As the gravy simmered, Jack entered his office. No email yet from Emerson, who had promised information on Marta Pacheco. Jack assumed he was asking her for permission. No matter. Via LinkedIn, Jack had her email address, her office location and phone number, and several photos. And age: She was sixty-nine. Katy would've been sixty-five had she survived.

Molly arrived shortly before seven. The scent of the gravy welcomed her before Jack could.

"Oh, that is just heavenly." She sniffed the fragrant air again. "When is the last time you made pasta?"

Jack came out of his office. "We were mere children." Cheek pecks; Molly ran her hand along Jack's shoulder.

A large green salad with fennel and Manzanilla olives waited on the marble counter. Jack had defrosted a half-loaf of ciabatta bread.

Molly went off to the bedroom and emerged in a black turtleneck sweater and jeans.

The cork of the bottle of Sangiovese surrendered with a pop. Jack poured a mouthful and swirled it. "You want to taste?" he said, as he came around the counter, glass in hand.

She accepted the Italian red. "Mmm," she said as she sipped. "Princeton was good, I gather."

"Good," he confirmed. "Nice man. Possibilities."

"Say more."

"Gay singer-songwriter, a promising talent thwarted in New York, sets out for Nashville, returns and plunges from a rooftop a short walk from country music's northern citadel."

"Well," she said. "I'd read that."

There were countless holes, Jack knew, but that never bothered him. Holes needed to be filled with facts. Facts obtained by working the story.

"Water's boiling," Molly said, pointing toward the stove.

Associated Music was on 54th Street, off Eighth, up a steep flight of stairs in a building that had fought off the theatre district's chomp-chomp gentrification.

Associated had made its money by transcribing charts for orchestras and smaller combos. Much of their work had been swallowed up by computer programs that could do the same task, so Sid and Sylvia Rosensaft set out to find new sources of income. When Colony Music, the last of the Tin Pan Alley music stores on Broadway, shut down in 2012, Sid bought their massive inventory of sheet music and started an online mail-order business.

He kept some of the sheets on creaking skeleton shelves behind the counter, others in boxes and crates from floor to ceiling in an already overstuffed shop.

Another act of diversification by the Rosensafts was to set up an operation that converted old vinyl, cassettes and CDs into digital files.

Katy's cassettes rattled as Jack plopped his sack on the counter.

He was greeted by a man with a bushy salt-and-pepper mustache. Rotund, but not flabby, he wore a navy sweater vest over a pale blue dress shirt and navy slacks. As he drew nearer, Jack could detect the scent of a cigar.

"Sid Rosensaft?"

"Sid Rosensaft," the man repeated.

Thinking Associated Music a tired, dusty remnant from Tin Pan Alley's glory days, Jack expected Rosensaft to be in his 80s and made cranky by a lifetime of mercantile drudgery while his former peers vanished. But Rosensaft was younger than Jack and he shone brightly, as if running the shop was better than free donuts.

"I need some cassettes converted to files." Jack took them out of the bag.

"Do you own the music?" Rosensaft asked.

Jack said no. "These are homemade recordings by a kid. A teen."

Rosensaft examined the plastic cases.

"Long ago. Could be as early as 1968."

"Katherine Emerson. Katy Emerson," said Rosensaft, reading aloud. "Family?"

"Subject," he said, "maybe."

Rosensaft tilted his head in confusion.

"She was a singer in the 1970s. Folk, maybe some modest success. Her brother gave those to me."

Jack introduced himself.

"Sure. The critic. *The New National Observer*. You do good work. I can't afford a subscription, though. But you're writing a book now?"

Hmmm, thought Jack. Rosensaft had inadvertently proposed a way for him to explain why he was looking into a folk singer no one had talked about in decades.

"Could be," Jack said, neither lying nor telling the truth.

Leaning an elbow on the counter, Sid Rosensaft told Jack he, too, was thinking of writing a book.

Jack looked around the tired old shop. The Rosensafts had kept it going through thin times. Maybe there was a story in their perseverance.

"No, not about this place," Sid said. "No. It was a thing that happened when I was a kid."

"What kind of thing?"

"I was in the back of a pickup, a Chevy, messing around with my friends, as kids do. We were on the Belt Parkway."

Jack grimaced in anticipation.

"I remember it so clearly. Blue Öyster Cult on the radio. We were doing fifty, at least fifty, and I got on my knees to move over, and we hit a pothole, and out I flew."

"Jesus," Jack said.

"I hit the highway and landed flat. A pickup truck ran over me, and then another one ran over me, and…nothing." He pointed to his chin. "A cut. Like a rug burn. Nothing else."

"It's a miracle," Jack said.

Rosensaft threw his hands in the air. "Yes! That's what I say. 'A miracle.' Don't you think people would want to read about that?"

"I do."

"You want to write it?"

"Well, by itself, it's not enough for a book, Mr. Rosensaft."

"Sid."

"It's an anecdote."

"You flesh it out."

"I'd better pass," Jack said, gesturing toward the cassettes. "I don't know how this thing will go."

Rosensaft nodded thoughtfully. "OK," he said finally. "You want files. WAV or MP3?"

Jack chose the latter. "Are the tapes fragile? I don't know. I didn't look at them."

Snapping open a plastic case, Rosensaft examined the cassette. With the tip of a pencil, he tugged on the tape. "We'll be fine. No problem. When do you need them by?"

Jack said there was no rush. "What works for you?"

"Come back tomorrow afternoon."

Jack agreed. Dipping into his pocket, he pulled out a thumb drive in the shape of a Fender Jaguar guitar.

"Cute," Rosensaft said.

"I got it at some convention. Is there any chance you could email me if you come across a song called 'Camera'?"

Scrunching his face, he said, "I don't listen to these things. Are you kidding? You've got five sixty-minute cassettes here."

"Doesn't mean there's five hours of music."

"You want copies, you'll get copies."

"Fair enough." He passed the bag to Rosensaft. "Pay now?"

"What? I can't trust the mighty *Observer*? Come by tomorrow."

Jack said he would.

Chapter Six

Marta Pacheco agreed to meet him at a restaurant near Lincoln Center, an upscale neighborhood staple that had cane chairs, leather banquettes, and a tower of fresh shellfish on display. When Jack arrived, the breakfast crowd had thinned out and the room was almost empty. He located her easily.

"Marta?" he said. She wore a red-and-beige paisley wrap across the shoulder of her brown suit jacket.

She shook his hand without enthusiasm, her fingers knotted with a trace of arthritis. A stern expression covered her wide face, and there was something like anger in her dark eyes.

In the awkward silence, Jack said, "OK if I sit?"

She nodded with indifference.

He put his notebook on the table as he removed his leather coat. "Thank you for agreeing to see me."

He could have sworn she grunted in disapproval.

Jack was well-accustomed to subjects who tried to establish dominance. One-word answers, eye-rolling condemnations of questions deemed beneath reply, snorting refusals to accept well-established premises, and pouting worthy of a trust-fund bully were all indications that the subject had something to conceal.

"Mr. Fiorello…"

"Let's make it Jack, OK?"

He took his seat and hopped it toward the table. She was drinking coffee. When the waitress appeared, Jack asked for an iced tea.

"What do you want, Mr. Fiorello?"

"Don Emerson thought it might be a good idea if we spoke."

She lifted her cup and stared over its lip.

He said, "So how about we speak?"

"I repeat: What is your interest in me?"

"Could be none," he replied. "It's early days. Either there's a story in Katy or there isn't."

"What kind of story?" she asked.

"You tell me. I enter through the music. Is there more to it?"

She replied with a condescending smile.

As he waited, Jack said nothing. Marta Pacheco couldn't know that Jack was not so much patient as not there. He was in the crowd as the Who played Leeds, then in the passenger's seat as Compay Segundo drove a big ol' Ford Fairlane along the Malecón. At Chalice in Hollywood, he watched as Kendrick Lamar shared a laugh with Robert Glasper at a grand piano.

"That was a very long time ago," she said directly.

A tall glass of iced tea was at his elbow. "For me, that's not so. I had never come across her music until recently. I still haven't heard her sing. When I do, it will be brand new."

"You'll never find her."

Oh, you'd be surprised. "Tell me. You were her friend, her roommate. She's in her room, guitar on her lap, notebook nearby or maybe a cassette recorder. She's working to get the song right. The right phrase, the right chord. They're elusive, but she's determined. Are you there? Where are you?"

"Why not ask the question you came to ask?" she said.

"Which one was that?"

"Please, Mr. Fiorello. I'm not one of your little rock stars who want to see their name in your newspaper."

"Well, that's not very nice."

She leaned in. "Whatever happened had nothing to do with us."

Jack heard it. "'Us'? You were together?"

"Oh, please. You know, you're not much of a reporter—"

He had assumed so but needed her to say it. "I didn't know. Don didn't tell me."

She stared at him. "It's no one's business now."

"Of course not," Jack said. "I tell you in all sincerity that I'm only interested in Katy Shayne as a songwriter who died before her time. I read the words to 'Camera' and a verse from a song she may not have even finished. Herm Odell said she could write. That's it."

She was unmoved.

"Did we lose a promising artist at age twenty-four? If you say yes, I'm going to ask, how do you know."

"Because I was with someone who would never have surrendered," she replied sharply. Rapping the tabletop with an index finger, she added, "She would not accept failure."

"Was she facing failure?"

"What you don't know, Mr. Fiorello."

"Multitudes," he said. "I don't know multitudes. But tell me. What happened?"

She hesitated. "No. I don't think I will."

"She would have never surrendered. Yet she commits suicide? I don't—"

"This is what I feared. No. I won't open old wounds. I am not a sadist. And Katy deserves peace."

He said, "She may deserve more than that. Many artists achieve their life's ambitions after they've passed."

"So what do you need from me? Do you want me to say I was devastated? You want to find us in those songs?"

"Are you in those songs?"

"You say you understand. If you do, you will stop. For me, nothing good can come of this. I lost her forty years ago. I have a life of my own."

Jack hesitated. "I can't conceal that Katy was gay, Marta. I can call you a friend, if need be."

"And the inference…?"

"Yes. There's that."

He knew it was time to withdraw. Often, he would allow a subject to ponder their initial reaction, then follow up by phone or email.

Jack withdrew a $5 bill from his wallet and put it on the table. He wriggled into his coat.

"I didn't mean to upset you," he said. "I'll leave you be. If you change your mind…"

She stared into her coffee cup.

A light snow was falling on Broadway. Hands in his pockets, Jack looked this way and that. Over in the Lincoln Center plaza, the water of the Revson Fountain danced unperturbed. A bus pulled in front of Avery Fisher Hall. Soon, tourists began to disembark. Puzzled but no less determined, he headed south to midtown.

After leaving Associated Music with files of Katy's music, Jack stopped for a late lunch and, as the sun began to fade, set up at the 42nd Street branch of the New York Public Library. For background, he read articles on microfiche about the stirrings of the gay pride movement and the 1969 Stonewall riots to get a sense of the environment in which Katy lived and worked.

Jack knew many gay musicians, but he tried to recall who among women singer-songwriters had come out back then. At the moment, he could think of no one. The bias was thick and unforgiving. While Bowie, Marc Bolan, the New York Dolls, and others were playing up their androgynous images, women had to work straight. It wasn't until close to her death that Jack found out Dusty Springfield was gay or, as she put it, "bent"; Dusty Springfield, whose smoky delivery on the first verse of "Son of A Preacher Man" was about the sexiest thing he'd ever heard.

Back downtown, Jack found the streets had emptied. The wind howled without shame. When he entered the apartment, he saw Molly had a rotisserie chicken and sides on the counter.

Jack kissed her cheek.

"Did you talk to Suzi?"

He laid Katy's material by the office door and shook off his coat, if not the chill. "Reading. Research. Katy Shayne."

On her way to the bedroom, Molly stopped to lower the window shades.

"You seem miffed." Using dish soap, he washed his hands in the kitchen sink.

She said, "Things are hectic. I may be going back to Chad. Oxfam hit us up with an RFP."

Request for Proposal. "Hit you up, huh?"

She sat on her stool at the counter. Jack carved the chicken and slid a plate toward Molly. Then, he cut a few slices for himself. He could smell the mesquite rise from the crispy skin.

"You'd tell me if you were upset…"

"Jack, if I were upset, would I have to tell you? After all these years?"

"You would conceal to make it easier for me," he said, as he settled at the counter's rounded corner. "We share that trait. Admit it."

"You love to do that: Manipulate me into a position where I have to agree with you."

"Yeah, what a way to make a living…"

They ate in silence. The kale salad was soggy, but the roasted potatoes were still warm. They shared the last of the Sangiovese from the other night.

"Katy Shayne," Molly said. "To what end?"

"To see. To find out. I've got the time now. There's not ten albums to listen to every day anymore. No two shows a night."

Pointing with her knife tip, she said, "You don't do anything without a reason. We both know that."

"I thought you'd be pleased. I'm not sitting around wallowing and moaning and trying to guess which musician will die next."

Molly eyed him with suspicion.

"What?"

"You're agreeing to write the IMs. You're going to be positioned to publish a collection of your columns. Prioritize," Molly told him. "Call Suzi."

He moaned.

Later, as she loaded the dishwasher, Molly said, "You can apply for Social Security, you know."

They had agreed to hold off on SSI until Molly retired. Jack had intended to work at *The Observer* until he dropped. He joked that they would find his body in a Porta Potty two days after a festival ended.

"I'd like to see that you have a plan, Jack. That's all."

Jack had the beginnings of a plan. A sketch. An inkling.

She dried her hands and tossed aside the dish towel. "Your reputation belongs to you. And you have a right to whatever income it might generate. How would you feel if you found out *The Observer* was going to publish a collection of your work?"

He shrugged.

"Don't," she said. "You'd be mad as hell. But they could do it."

"Is that what Suzi said? They want to do that?"

Jack saw a publication party at a bookstore in midtown. A big celebration. Many former colleagues. Publicists. Balloons and streamers. Would you care to say a few words, Jack?

He said, "They wouldn't do that."

"You didn't think they would let you go on the day you turned sixty-five." She went toward the sofa. "The point is, if you get this right, it will appear that you left on your own terms."

"Do you think I give a damn how it appears? Really? Is that me? Why are you pushing this?"

"Close the deal, Jack. We're talking about your reputation. And income. What are we doing here? I'm arguing for you. You won't move."

Jack closed his eyes and hung his head. Then he was watching Jonny Greenwood testing his pedals, his beat-up Telecaster emitting otherworldly chords. The rest of Radiohead lingered by Phil Selway's drums. Thom Yorke was spinning a story. From the side of the stage, Jack couldn't hear him.

"Call Suzi now. She's waiting."

"Tomorrow," he said.

Jack slept through Molly's alarm, and it was 9:30 before he gathered himself to get out of bed. He lumbered to the bathroom, hamstrings tight, his mind encased in clouds.

There was a Post-It note from Molly on the bathroom mirror. "I'm sorry. It wasn't you. Lunch?"

Clearing his throat, he said, "Can't." He grabbed his toothbrush. "Busy."

Jack retrieved his phone from the nightstand and IMed Molly, declining her invitation.

She responded immediately. "Mad?"

"Who could stay mad at you?" he typed quickly. Then he crossed out "stay" and replaced it with "be."

"Chad is on," she replied. "Maybe."

"Today?" He had a towel around his waist.

"If so, soon."

In an email, Don Emerson admitted to melancholy in his Princeton office. At home, he remembered how much he missed his sister. He took out the family photo album, an experience he called "bittersweet, as always." Jack pictured sadness around a crackling fire, Betty holding Don's hand in sympathy.

Carrying coffee, Jack settled in at his desk. Nudging aside his laptop, he displayed Katy's pick, her capo, the turquoise earrings and the necklace with its heart-shaped pendant.

"Katy," he said aloud, "I'm going to run a few things by you."

Why not? He'd spoken to deceased subjects of his *Observer* column, asking Max Roach if he properly understood his "We Insist!" when it was reissued after his death. Last year, he said to Gregg Allman, "Did I do you justice?" when he wrote his IM. Jack heard no replies but somehow felt they approved.

He held up Katy's childhood notebook. "I found some really interesting stuff in here. Do you remember? Your manifesto: very touching, Katy. 'I will let the world know who I am and what I feel with my songs. I will sing them loudly and with pride.' With an exclamation point. You were what? Twelve, thirteen when you wrote it? You were beginning to know who you were and what you wanted."

He might've added that, by the time he reached his teens, Jack also knew how he was going to escape: He would become someone who would help readers find refuge and deeper meaning in popular music, as he had begun to. That old song he heard as he did his homework in his bedroom while his shrieking mother hectored his father and then scalded him with a hot iron as he bathed? Jack could call it up right this minute and could hear it as clearly as he did in his gray, boxy room with a finger in one ear and a little white earplug in the other. Back then, he wasn't yet able to slide himself into a safe place, but soon, there would be days when he would hear only the song and not his parents' screams. Did the police come and take his mother away? Did Jack ride in the ambulance with his father as it tore toward the emergency room? He couldn't recall. But he remembered hearing the song and wanting to share what he knew. Earl Palmer played drums, Carol Kaye and Ray Pohlman were on bass. People think Jack Nitzsche arranged it, but no. It was Gene Page. Bobby Hatfield and Bill Medley sang it like they each had a dagger in their hearts. "You've Lost That Lovin' Feeling" was a desperate plea from a man who knew her love would never return, but the record didn't make Jack Fiorello sad. Its majesty ushered him to a sanctuary where miracles occurred. That kind of thing happened again and again. Bursting through his desolation, a song arrived. Jack listened carefully and he was saved.

To Katy, he now said, "You were probably wise to avoid writing specifically about your sexuality, at least directly, in a book your classmates or parents might have found. 'I will sing with pride,' says enough.

"And the song 'Camera.' You were in high school when you wrote that? I'm no flatterer. Katy, but that was heady stuff for a kid."

Flipping the pages, he located the lyrics in the notebook and read them aloud:

"She smiles for a while as the photo is taken / But she cannot conceal what she feels / They're so badly mistaken…"

He said, "In waltz time? I like the defiance at the end. That little twist. 'I cannot control what I feel. I cannot control what I feel. I will not control what I feel…' The ellipsis is a nice touch. You wanted it to fade out."

Now, Jack took up her yearbook. "Math Club, but you received an award in poetry. It's all rhythm, right?

"And I see you went to your prom. Jesus, Katy you're a foot taller than…Carl. But it's great. Very Sixties." He thought, Your look is somewhere between

Judy Collins and Morticia Adams.

Opening his laptop, he pushed in the guitar-shaped thumb drive and tapped a few keys. Rosensaft had labeled the five files "Cassette One," "Cassette Two," and so on.

"Katy, let's listen, OK?"

In his iTunes player, Jack clicked on "Cassette One."

With a peep, a young girl said, "This song is called 'Mary Street.' Written and performed by Katherine Emerson."

Seconds later, the song began with a chugging G chord that was all but identical to the opening of "The Times They Are a-Changin.'" Soon, she traced Dylan's chord pattern: G-Em-C-G, then G-Em-C-D. That's fine, thought Jack. Twenty-two when he wrote it, Dylan borrowed from British folk ballads; a key line was lifted from the Book of Ecclesiastes.

Katy's melody followed the chords, but differed from Dylan's, which had a hypnotic cadence that suited the apocalyptic messages. Katy's "Mary Street" was an overstuffed torrent of words, a screed against a narrow-minded small town that would not let its children become who they wanted to be. As if to comment on her thesis, a car horn bleated in the distance as she began the fifth of 14 verses.

As the song ended, Katy let the final chord ring through the tape's hiss, then reached over and clicked off the machine.

"Was that your Guild D-40?" Jack asked. If so, she might've recorded the track as early as '68 when she was 15. If not, she might have been younger. Either way, she was advanced in both the sturdy confidence of her chording and, more so, in her use of language.

He clicked on "Cassette Two."

On tape, Katy announced, "This is 'You Didn't Have to Be So Nice' written by Steve Boone and John Sebastian and arranged and performed by Katherine Emerson."

If the tape hiss was similar, Katy's speaking voice was more assertive. She made this well after "Mary Street," Jack thought.

The mid-tempo performance opened with Katy finger-picking an A chord. She then introduced the lyric in a soothing yet bittersweet manner.

Jack knew the song well. It was a gentle frolic of a love song about finding the right girl at the right time. But Katy's reading had the air of a wish rather than an inevitability, reflecting a fleeting moment that may have never been realized.

Quite an interpretation by a teenager. Jack was genuinely moved.

"Beautiful, Katy," he said. "I hope you did something with it."

"Cassette Three" was a flop. Apparently, Katy had come across Joni Mitchell's "Blue," and she decided she needed to diversify. She played her own composition "That Didn't Last Too Long" on piano—badly, working triads with her right hand and the root note in a lower register. The song was in E, not the best key for piano anyway, but it might've worked on guitar with a little bit of a country bounce to it. At the bridge, she went to a G# instead of the expected G#m, and that worked fine. But without needed energy, it sort of just lay there.

"Blah," said Jack. "Song is salvageable, but the arrangement… Sorry, Katy."

"Camera" was on the fourth cassette and it was a big winner. Arranged and sung as if it had its roots in pre-1960s folk, Katy played her guitar with the capo at the fifth fret. Her playing was flawless and Jack was reminded that the simplest things are often the hardest to pull off.

She retained the first line from her notebook: "She smiles for a while as the photo is taken / But she cannot conceal what she feels / They're so badly mistaken."

Now that Jack knew young Katy was coping with her sexuality in a hostile environment, the story took on an added poignancy. Though she used the third person, Katy was singing about herself—and she was proud to be who she was and wasn't seeking anyone's approval. It was a heck of an achievement for a teen—a precise, mature composition that more than spoke of Katy's promise: At least for one song, her potential had been realized.

"Terrific, Katy. Just lovely in every way."

Jack listened to it again immediately, this time focusing on Katy's voice. It was true, not at all pitchy, but underdeveloped. Bel canto female singers like Baez and Collins had set a high bar for folk in the '60s. Young Katy's voice wasn't there yet. Perhaps to compensate, she emphasized the poignant yet ultimately defiant nature of the lyric, holding tones above certain phrases and spitting out others, her sort-of-pretty voice growing harsher as the song progressed. Those were smart, savvy choices.

Keeping his criticism to himself, he said, "My question is, what did you do with it? I'm thinking only you could've pulled it off. Did you?" With a smile, he added, "Not in the mood for a conversation?"

Waiting for Katy's pick across the guitar strings on Cassette Five, Jack sipped his lukewarm coffee.

"Hi, this is Katy Shayne."

Startled, Jack put down his cup.

"The songs you'll hear are intended to give you a sense of what I can do."

Her speaking voice had lost its little-girl lilt. She spoke directly, confidently. Jack turned to the open yearbook. Tall girl, long black hair, dark eyes, high cheekbones, rounded chin and a dimple. It took no effort to imagine she was standing at his office door.

"I consider myself a songwriter, but I love to sing a great tune no matter who composed it and no matter when it was composed. My goal is to work with the best people, put together a great band and, with Greenwich Village as my home, get my music across to anyone who needs to hear it."

"Needs to hear it," thought Jack. Hmmm. Interesting positioning. Share my journey with me. I'm on your side.

You had a plan, didn't you, Katy?

"Thank you so much for listening to my music. I look forward to meeting you and hearing what you have to say.

"Have a great one. Bye."

Over the silence, Jack said, "Did they get back to you, Katy? They should have. Were I in A&R at a record company back then, I would've bet on you."

As he shut his laptop, he said, "How am I going to hear what you sounded like after you left Hopewell? Did you cut any demos in New York? What about your band? Did it happen?"

Jack waited, but there was no reply.

To make nice, Jack sent the "Camera" file to Marta Pacheco; he didn't mention their mid-morning tension. "Thought you might enjoy this," he wrote, signing the email Jack G., then erasing his middle initial.

Sending every file to Don Emerson, he wrote: "Very impressive. She was right to believe in herself."

Molly's trip to Chad was on. After a few nice minutes of quiet time together, they went to dinner in the neighborhood, a casual sushi place. They weren't adventurous when choosing sushi and sashimi. Jack liked spicy tuna, Molly salmon. She was deft with chopsticks; with Jack, it was like spearfishing.

When she asked about his day, he kept it breezy: Katy's music—very promising for a kid. He told her a bit about Marta. Their brief meeting gave Katy a new dimension and brought her into sharper focus. In Marta, Jack saw passion in a fiery lover who still cherished her memories decades later.

"Chad," Jack said, as they set aside the menus. "What's the project?"

"The next generation of anti-malaria netting. The WHO acknowledges that it would be an improvement, but not at the current price. So health officers in Africa are reluctant—forbidden, actually—to buy them. Chad said no. We need to save lives. Our economy is devastated."

"How do you get to…?"

"N'Djamena," she said between sips of rosé. "Via Dubai. With a layover, it's about twenty-two or twenty-three hours."

"Plus the time it takes to get to Geneva."

"There's that."

"So, how long will you be gone?"

She said, "Ten days."

"Ten? Wow. You'll miss Thanksgiving. We've never spent Thanksgiving apart."

"I'm thinking I have to do this, Jack. It's a good project. Protection is available if the governments will cooperate."

Their plates arrived. Molly's salmon glistened. Jack struggled to align the chopsticks in his hand.

"It looks like I'll be leaving on Monday."

"Do you want to do something before you go?" he asked. "A drive? You like the beach in the winter."

"I need the weekend to prep. But do something special, Jack. Give yourself a treat."

Jack nodded thoughtfully. His treat: to suss out what to do about Katy Shayne, who was determined and who would not surrender—but who killed herself a half block from the Lone Star Café with a Nashville phone number in her purse.

On Monday, they said their goodbyes over a hurried breakfast. A car service waited down on Broadway.

"Be good," Jack said.

"Go see Suzi," she replied. "And don't spend Thanksgiving alone."

They shared a long hug and a short kiss.

He rolled her bag down to the lobby. Well-underdressed in a hoodie, Jack waved as the black limousine pulled away from the building and into the crawling traffic.

Chapter Seven

With Klee's "Tänzerin" and "Fleeing Ghost" looking on, Jack dialed Suzi from the living-room sofa.

"Sorry I haven't gotten back to you," he said.

She waited as if he was going to offer an excuse.

"*The Observer* is amendable to our request," she said finally.

"What do I have to do?"

There were documents he needed to sign.

"You might want to thank Mr. Reinhard," she added. "I sense that he hated to see you go. He took up the torch."

Must be a legal term.

She suggested they meet for lunch at Remembering Leo, a Cajun restaurant near the Flatiron Building, which sits snugly where Fifth Avenue and Broadway intersect.

"Who's buying?" he said.

"One way or another," she replied, "it's always the client."

He decided to walk the two miles uptown despite the battering wind. Folding into the restaurant crowd, Jack settled in a booth in back. He ordered an iced tea and checked his email. Wrote Don Emerson: "Thank you so much, Jack. I hadn't heard her songs in years. She was good, wasn't she?'

"Very promising," Jack replied.

Nothing from Marta.

A decade ago, Jack had lunch at Remembering Leo with Wardell Quezergue, the anointed Creole Beethoven who had worked with just about every New Orleans artist including Fats Domino, the Nevilles and Dr. John. Quezergue, who was blind, came in, inhaled long and deep, and then smiled knowingly. When he died in 2011, Jack wrote an IM, but Reinhard spiked it. "Reflected light," he told Jack, proving how little he knew about how hit records were made.

Suzi arrived in a cherry-red down coat that ended just above her zebra chukka boots. She removed her pink stocking cap and shook out her hair; Jack stood, and they air-kissed; Suzi went "mwop." He took her coat to a hook on the wall near a photo of somewhere deep in the murky bayou.

"Aren't you bright?" Jack said as he slipped back into the booth.

She wore a neon-orange knee-length dress and a spiky silver necklace that scooped down her neckline. Her dozen or so bracelets jingle-jangled.

"Did you order?" she asked as she settled in. "Let's fortify. I'm famished."

Jack read the specials on the chalkboard on a far wall. When the waiter came by, he ordered shrimp and grits, Suzi the boudin noir plate. They agreed to share a side of fried okra.

"A lawyer having flesh and blood for lunch. Well, well…"

"Clever, Jack." She dropped a manila folder on the table. "It's good to get this done. Really. Move on, you know?"

There were yellow arrow stickers on the documents to indicate where he had to sign.

Jack thumbed through the pages. "Am I OK with this?"

She wiped her glasses on the napkin. "I've done a lot of termination agreements, Jack. It's boilerplate, but the copyrights are yours. So that's better than OK—if you're going to do something with them."

Jack looked at her. "How long do I have before I'm finished at the paper?"

"That's not in the agreement. That's between you and your editor. What did you say? There were sixty-seven names on your list. It's not a matter of 'how long' then, is it? It's until the sixty-seventh musician dies."

He said, "I can do three a day if I'm not invested."

"And if you're invested?"

"Then it hurts. I'm not writing about entertainment. I'm writing about an artist who changed lives, who was courageous. Someone admirable. I have to manage my emotions—but not too much."

"Do the ones you don't care about first. Develop a routine."

Jack said, "Routine: Guy is dead. Made hits long ago. You remember him. No? Here's some background bio. Guy hasn't done a damned thing worthwhile in forty years. Your relationship with him is unchanged. Are you sorry your youth has flown away? That you'll die too? Is that it?"

"That's cruel, Jack. It's not you."

He sighed. "You're right. I actually do respect the grief. Music means so much to us, doesn't it? The uplift, the prompt to introspection. Joy. Sorrow. It's no surprise that we want to hold on to those who made us feel… Who made us feel."

"Is that how you're feeling, Jack? Your youth has flown away?"

"Not until my sixty-fifth birthday. My sweet bird was in full flight and I was never, ever going to die."

Suzi leaned in. "Go on, Jack. It's all right."

He shook his head. "Nah…"

"Really. Tell me. Make me see what it was like."

Jack hesitated. Then, with a wave of his hand, he said, "Inside the music, Suzi, when it's in you and around you and you're with artists who are achieving or trying to achieve—talented, hard-working people, incredibly dedicated people, long-suffering. Through them, you see the future of music. You don't get old. Your life is renewed."

"And you can't have that anymore?"

"I can't have that anymore."

"I don't know how to respond," she said. "Maybe go talk to someone, you know? A therapist. A counselor."

"I think I'll say no. They'll try to tell me I'm wrong. I'm not wrong." He signed his name on the first dotted line. "I'm thinking they will tell me to revel in what I've done. To be satisfied. Accept." He signed again.

Suzi said, "Now, the other one. Sign."

"How's our Henry Lee?" Jack asked.

"Oh, Henry is steady. Henry is good."

"'Good' is in 'fine,' 'not sick?' Or 'good' as in 'pure of heart?'"

She laughed. "Both. He's good. And good. You should call him. He digs you."

"'He digs me?'"

"He said that. Those words."

"Well, tell him I dig him too," Jack said as he returned the first document.

"Take him to a show. He'd love that."

Another signature.

"I'm curious, Jack," she said. "You're a little bit impenetrable. Do you have friends?"

"Don't be mean."

Her bracelets rattled as she gestured. "Do you hang with the guys? Play poker? Talk sportsball, cars, whatever?"

Jack started signing the second copy. "I like people," he said.

"All of a sudden, I'm thinking how little I know about you."

Jack laughed. "There may not be much more than you know. Me and Molly, and I was the rock-and-pop critic of *The New National Observer*."

"What were you like as a kid?"

"Invisible. Intentionally so. You can figure out how I learned to deflect."

The food arrived. Suzi's blood sausages rested on a bed of dirty rice. Jack savored the steaming scent of his boiled shrimp.

"Let the good times roll," Jack said, by way of a toast.

Suzi ate with appealing gusto. "I think of Molly as a friend," she said. "You and I, are we friends?"

"Tell me how to answer that." The buttery grits were perfect.

She chuckled. "I'm not going to beg, Jack."

"Look, Suzi, I appreciate you. And Henry. I do. But let me tell you: With me, there's no there there. To be a critic is to be on the outside—not a musician and not a fan. That suited me: I was a world of one. And when I came home, there was Molly. Now it's all out of whack. Tilted."

Jack put down his fork and picked up the pen. Giancarlo Fiorello, again and then again. He was certain not a single *Observer* reader knew the G in his byline stood for his legal name. His mother, who was threatened and exposed by the warmth of her husband's family, detested the name his father had chosen. She began calling him Jack when he was still in the incubator.

"I get that you're shook, but don't fall to self-pity. I've got clients that unless I get them something, they will vanish," she said. "They were terminated without cause and they haven't got enough money to make this month's rent. I have a woman with three kids who was fired because she wouldn't suck off her boss under his desk. Now she's diagnosed with Parkinson's. No insurance. Try to remember that *The New National Observer* is offering you a deal as a freelancer and giving you the rights to your articles. Plus severance and insurance."

"You're saying they flung me from a moving car and I landed on soft grass."

"Be better. That's all. They like you. I like you; Henry, too. And Molly loves you."

He pushed the signed agreements across the table. "Suzi, how important is it to you to be a lawyer? 'Hey, look, there goes Shoshana Epstein-Lee. She is one killer lawyer. You need an attorney, you can't do better than Suzi Lee.' Sweet, right?"

"In context. But I'm Jill's Mom, too. A good partner to Henry. I self-amuse. I knit like a motherfucker, Jack. I'm saying: 'Integrate.'"

"Say, 'do, Jack. 'Go do.'"

"Go do."

"Do you know that song 'Go Do' by Jónsi from Sigur Rós? 'You and the sunrise will never fall under. We should always know that dreams can do everything.'"

"Lovely," she said.

"I had dinner with him and the guys in Reykjavik. Then they took me to see Björk in the round. That will never happen again."

"The song, though. It's still there. And you just gave it to me." Before he could reply, she said, "Jack, go home and blast your favorite album. Dance around the house. The music—take it back. Make it yours again. Whatever works for you."

"Katy Shayne," he said.

"Who?"

"Nothing. Never mind."

"Let's enjoy the meal. Two friends, OK?"

"No worries," he told her.

"Come on, Jack. You can do it."

Back home, Jack hung up his coat, wrapping his scarf around the hanger. The apartment was as empty as it had ever been. He went to the window, pulled back the curtain, and looked down. The world was still there, curiously silent.

He took his laptop to the kitchen counter. His stomach was reminding him that spicy food wasn't always his friend. Gastroesophageal Reflux Disease. GERD. Who hears of such a thing? Apparently, seniors do.

He was thinking about Katy Shayne. Such promise. Then dead at 24. At 24, Jack was clay waiting to be molded. It was all possible, every bit of it. Time was everlasting.

But not for Katy. It all ended when she was that age. Why? Depression. Cruel judgment. Betrayal.

He said, "All those years, Katy. They were denied to you. All those songs...

"I had my life, didn't I? You never did. You fought for it, you worked so damned hard, you were almost there, Katy. And then..."

He clicked on a file.

Over the hiss on the tape, a very young Katy said, "This is 'Camera,' written and performed by Katherine Emerson..."

Soon, she sang, "She smiles for a while as the photo is taken / But she cannot conceal what she feels / They're so badly mistaken."

Jack closed his eyes to listen.

Splayed on the sofa, his ratty robe over his T and jeans, Mollyless Jack flipped through the movie channels. It was growing late, nearly 11 o'clock, and he'd yet to have dinner. As he slouched toward the kitchen, his phone buzzed in his pocket.

It was an IM from a 212 number he didn't recognize.

"Thank you. I suggest you call Carpenter," it read.

Jack typed his reply. "Marta? He is...?"

"Alan Carpenter. A.A. He plays the guitar."

By now, Jack was in his office, Google open and waiting.

A.A. Carpenter worked in a guitar shop on the Lower East Side.

"Can I see you again?" Jack asked Marta.

She wrote, "Yes, you may."

Jack called Eldridge Guitars moments before it was scheduled to open.

"Is A.A. around?" he asked.

"Me," Carpenter replied.

"Jack Fiorello, *The Observer*. I'm working on a thing and I hear you can help."

"The newspaper? You're a reporter?"

"Want to grab lunch?"

"I haven't had breakfast yet."

"Musicians' hours," Jack said. "How about two o'clock?"

Carpenter suggested a casual burger joint on Houston.

"Then and there," Jack replied.

Two hours later, Jack and his red notebook were waiting in a plastic booth. He nursed a Snapple. On Houston, a jackhammer was ripping through blacktop. Orange cones redirected lurching traffic.

Carpenter was a big man with a big beard. When he took down the hood on his heavy coat, he revealed a shaved head and two pirate earrings. Despite the Southern accent Jack detected on the phone, A.A. Carpenter looked like Williamsburg circa 2005. He hardly resembled the lean, cat-eyed guitarist Jack found in photos on the web.

They shook hands. Then Carpenter went to the counter, ordered three burgers, fries and a Brooklyn Lager. He returned with the cold longneck.

"Cheers," said Jack, holding up his iced tea.

Carpenter tugged on his beard. "So…what's up?"

"Katy Shayne. You knew her?"

He nodded. "Played with her now and again."

Jack said, "Fell into my lap. It's beginning to feel like a story. I was talking to Herm Odell—"

"That son of a bitch. Let me guess." He hid a burp behind his fist. "Good songwriter. Lesbian, so she wouldn't put out. She killed herself."

"He didn't say she was gay."

"Everybody who was working the Village back then knew Katy was gay. She didn't hide it."

The counterman brought over Carpenter's tray. The runny burgers smelled better than they looked.

"You were saying…" Jack had his notebook open, his pen ready to scrawl.

"I first met her in 1974. Maybe late 1973."

"Katy was twenty, twenty-one."

"That's about right." Carpenter destroyed a burger with three bites.

"Where did you meet her?"

"At a hootenanny at the Bitter End. Open-mike night. I was impressed. I told her she needed a second guitar and I was available."

"You still have that '59 Telecaster?"

It was a tactic Jack long used to let his subjects know that he wasn't a general-assignment reporter kicked over to the music beat.

Carpenter was nodding. "You know I used that Telly with Katy, right?

Jack shook his head. "I don't know much about her. I heard five demos and read a notebook. I've never seen a picture of her except in her high school yearbook."

"When she cleaned up, Katy looked like…what's her name? The chick in *The Partridge Family*. She could put on a big smile, super-cute, glow. You know Susanna Hoffs, the Bangles? That kind of sexy but wholesome thing."

Carpenter put away his third burger. He ate the string fries six at a time.

"Did you work a lot?"

"I don't know if I'd call it work—as in we got paid," said Carpenter as he gulped the last of his beer. "We were gigging around. Katy was stubborn. The folk thing was dying by then. Joni was doing jazz, Judy was doing show tunes. Bruce had arrived. CBGB was about to open. Katy wanted to do folk ballads."

As Carpenter spoke, Jack tried to place Katy in context in the New York scene in the '70s. The Village was winding down. Dylan was long gone. Carole King had moved to L.A. to record "Tapestry." In New York, Phoebe

Snow was gigging at the old Kenny's Castaway with blues numbers and hints of gospel and jazz. You couldn't compete with folk tunes.

"I got the impression she was trying to stretch," Jack said. "The story songs. Audrey Munson. The Kim Novak thing."

"Not her best," Carpenter said. "Though you couldn't tell her. Once she dug in, she was dug in as all get out. And I guess she was right to. Ain't nobody timid making it anyhow."

"No, that's a fact." Jack passed him a napkin.

"You want to hear us? Me and Katy?"

"Sure," Jack said. He sipped the last of his iced tea and wriggled out of the booth.

Carpenter lived in a squat, brick building, a holdover from when the Lower East Side was a refuge for old-timers, struggling artists and kids trying to hang on in New York. Next door to his place was an eight-story glass-and-steel tower, needle-thin and singularly indistinct, that sold out before it was finished, with 600-foot apartments going for millions.

Carpenter's boots thudded on the shaky stairwell as Jack climbed with him to the third floor, passing doors coated with chipped paint, fixtures with exposed wires, lights that flickered evenly rather than burned steady.

They entered Carpenter's living room, which had a threadbare couch much like the one on the "Crosby, Stills & Nash" album cover, a coffee table studded with empty beer bottles and a crumbled sack from the burger joint they just left, and a TV so old it might as well have had an antennae. But over in the corner, he had a set-up for his gear on a well-worn Oriental rug: that gorgeous '59 Telecaster, a pricey Taylor acoustic guitar, a variety of pedals, a Nord keyboard, a couple of microphones on stands, a nice pair of speakers, and the obligatory MacBook, no doubt loaded with a digital audio workstation.

"Nice set-up," said Jack. He kept his coat on, but unzipped. There was little heat in the flat. "Are you still playing out?"

"Not too often," he replied as he fidgeted with his laptop.

"Recording?"

"The work's dried up. I haven't done a session in I don't know how long. So, yeah, I've been doing my own thing. Probably should've started sooner on that."

Jack sat on the arm of the wobbly sofa.

Carpenter popped his headphones from the laptop. "Found it. And here we go…"

Jack heard a smattering of applause. Then: "Hello. I'm Katy Shayne."

Somebody yelled, "Woo-woo."

"This is A.A., and this song is called 'Celia Remains.'"

She played a stark Em chord and a melodramatic D. Carpenter entered cautiously, making sure his electric guitar didn't overwhelm her acoustic. Soon, he offered a deft solo built around her riff on the D.

"There are five thousand love songs, five thousand loves / Carved in marble as pure as a dove / The songs of the poet bring joy and proclaim / No love is greater than when 'Celia Remains.'"

It was a melancholy folk tune and its only references to the music of the time were Carpenter's little licks that gave it a hint of country rock. But Katy's voice was stronger than it was on her bedroom tapes. When the duo arrived at the bridge, Katy's voice soared. "Come my Celia, why should we wait? / The time that is ours slowly decays," she sang powerfully, triumphantly.

Carpenter soloed briefly, using the melody as a guide. Soon, the song came to its close: "It's early in the evening, late in the day / The ships in the harbor have all sailed away / I sit on the deck and I write in the rain / While thoughts of loving Celia remain."

Over the applause, Jack said, "Nice. Cool tune. A big step forward, no? But not subtle: She's declaring her love for Celia."

Carpenter paused the sound. "She said some of the lines came from a poem. Seventeenth century? I don't rightly remember. That gave her a bit of cover if anybody asked."

"I liked it. You?"

"It's a good tune. But you can't move that thing. Ronstadt wasn't going to cover it. Maybe a guy like Richie Havens could've made it work. Fifteen years later, the Indigo Girls would've killed with it."

"She was writing for herself," Jack suggested.

"Sure. Like I said, she was stubborn." Carpenter stood. "Say, listen, I've got to get back to work—"

Jack stood, too. "No, this is just what I was looking for. Can you send me whatever you've got?" He wrote his email address on a page torn from his notebook.

Carpenter put it on his laptop keyboard. "You're planning to write about Katy for *The New National Observer*." He shook his head and chuckled as he shrugged into his heavy coat. "Ain't that the damnedest thing."

"Nothing's certain," Jack said. "If there's a story, it might not be right for *The Observer*. 'Promising Gay Folk Singer Kills Herself Four Decades Ago' isn't our style."

Carpenter opened the door to let Jack pass. As he secured the deadbolt, he said, "When she came back from Nashville, she was a mess. I used to say Katy went to Nashville, but Katy never came back."

Jack followed the big man down the stairs. "What kind of mess?"

"No spark," he said over his shoulder. "Kind of beaten, you know?"

They reached the ground floor. Carpenter tugged up his hood. "I was surprised, and I wasn't. Nashville can eat you alive. She had went all in. Cut ties and headed south."

Jack nodded. He wanted to take down what Carpenter was saying—there was good color in his choice of words—but he'd have to wait and recreate his quotes later.

"I always thought Katy would've been happy with a nice little house with a white picket fence and a little garden back somewhere in Jersey."

"Really? I heard she wanted to get out."

"Oh yeah. Like I wanted to get out of Alabama. But that kind of fuel only gets you so far. Once you get there, you realize you got to have more than anger and resentment to pull you through."

They stepped outside and began to walk toward Eldridge Street. The sky was a pale silver on its way to an early evening gray. With a handshake, Jack said goodbye to Carpenter.

"Hey, Jack. Mind if I send you some of my stuff?"

Ah, the reason for the information dump, the prattle and chatter. Quid pro quo.

"Great," Jack said. "Do." The only surprise in the request was that it hadn't come sooner.

Chapter Eight

Exiting the elevator in his Tribeca building, Jack found in the eighth-floor vestibule a bewildered deliveryman holding a pizza.

"How did you get in?" Jack asked.

"I push every buzzer," the man replied, his accent thick.

Behind him was a stairwell as wide as the one in Hitchcock's "Vertigo," with thick marble flights from the 13th floor down to the street-level landing. While waiting upstairs for the lift, Jack would peer over the waist-high rail and dizzy-spin away like Jimmy Stewart's Scottie, the agoraphobic ex-cop who was duped.

Jack pointed up, directing the deliveryman to the family at the far end of the ninth-floor hall.

When he entered his apartment, he ordered a pizza. An hour later, the deliveryman smiled when Jack opened the door. "You're an inspiration," Jack told him, upping the tip.

He watched a Barry Levinson double bill. When Carpenter failed to send the recordings by midnight, Jack drifted off on the sofa and stayed there. He dreamed that Natalie Merchant, in a navy jumpsuit, was pumping gas at a station outside Asheville, North Carolina, oily rag drooping out of her back pocket.

A little bit of sun peaking past the blinds crossed his face, waking him gently, pleasantly. He checked his phone before he lifted his head from his pillow. Molly had written from Geneva. All is well. "You're on your way to a new future, my dear one," she added.

"Talk tonight?" he typed. "Sooner?"

Jack brushed his teeth and dressed in yesterday's clothes.

"Going to breakfast," he told "Fleeing Ghost" and "Tänzerin."

At the diner, he ordered pancakes and, as he waited, ran through what Carpenter told him. It didn't add up. He said Katy was so determined to make it in Nashville that she left New York behind. What made her think she could succeed in Music City when she was struggling in New York, performing songs that were out of step with the times? Had she written new material better suited to country or country rock? Maybe the rest of the live set at the Bitter End Carpenter promised to send would tell.

He typed a message: "Don, why did your sister move to Nashville?"

The pancakes came just before Emerson's reply: "Opportunity? Will? I didn't know she was gone until she sent a postcard," he wrote.

"What did it say?"

"Nashville in big letters on the front like a travel poster. 'I'm here' on the back. And 'how's Roger?'"

"Roger?"

"Our pup. A little black terrier mix. The second Katy sat, Roger jumped right into her lap. Every time."

Now Jack had maple syrup between his fingers. He went to the restroom to wash up. When he returned, the remainder of his breakfast was gone—Jack the victim of an overzealous busboy.

Back home, he checked again for a message from Carpenter. Nothing. Then he banged out an email to the Press Relations office of the New York Police Department: "Can you tell me how I can do research on a cold case? A very cold case? Thanks so much."

One Police Plaza was nearby. He used to scoot around it on his way to Chinatown until a redheaded cop who looked about 12 years old chewed him out for hopping a concrete barrier as a shortcut. "Aren't you a little old for that, mister?" said the Baby Cop.

"Showering," Jack said now when he left his office. When he returned, clean and spiffy, he found in his inbox a reply from NYPD.

"Are you *the* Jack G.?" it began, "I didn't know rock critics covered crime. Or does this have to do with rock stars who died in NYC?"

The press officer included a phone number. A direct line, she said.

Jack dialed immediately.

"Jack G.!" the officer repeated with exaggerated cheer. "My Dad loves you. Every Christmas, he gives me the clippings of your columns and says those are the albums he wants."

"I like that," Jack said, who had paced to the kitchen. "Thanks."

"But he thinks you're losing your grip, Jack G. Hip-hop, techno, grime, sludge, mudge, whatever. Chamber music…where's the backbeat?"

"It's a big ol' world, isn't it?" Jack said. "Listen, Sergeant, I really don't know what I'm doing here. Is it possible you can keep this under your hat? I mean, don't tell the other guys what I'm on?"

"'The other guys' as in the other reporters?" She mentioned one who worked for *The Observer*'s New York section.

"If you don't mind," Jack said. "Am I asking too much?"

"Not at all," Sgt. Mary Donegal replied. "What's going on?"

Jack told her: reported suicide in 1977. The press said she jumped from a building on 13th Street. She was a musician, a singer-songwriter. He's intrigued. He started asking around. Maybe there's something in it.

"You know how it is," Jack added. "You're never sure if there's anything there."

"It was ruled a suicide?" she asked. Donegal had a slight speech impediment: "Suicide" came out as "shoishide."

"So said the *Daily News*."

"Then it's not a cold case, Jack G. It's closed."

Of course. "All right," he said, "but is there a file? I mean, maybe in the notes someone had some questions about whether it was suicide. I don't know…"

"You can request the file," she told him.

"Like I said, I don't know if I'm at the start of something or not."

"You can find a form online, Jack G. Fifteen dollars. But let me see what I can do."

"If it makes a difference, I'm like ten minutes from 1PP—"

"Slow down, Hopalong. Send me what you've got, and I'll see where we can go with it."

"Sorry. I'm eager, they tell me."

"Forget it. I'll get back asap." Ashap. "Got any good albums for my Dad?"

"What's he like?" Not mudge, I'm guessing.

"He's seen the movie 'The Last Waltz,' like, forty-two times."

Ah. He likes Scorsese's bloated pomp-and-circumstance take on the end of the Band, who were notable for their low-key, non-spectacle approach to music. "I'll put together a mix for you."

"Groovy, Jack G."

"Peace out, Sergeant."

Jack made his stuffing. He put it in a loaf tin and, along with a turkey breast, shoved it in the oven. He set a place for himself on the counter, and he opened a bottle of zinfandel. The scent of sage and roasting onions filled the flat.

It was mid-afternoon and surprisingly sunny. Without his coat, Jack went down to Broadway, where he stood in the middle of the street. He could see as far as the Chrysler Building two miles to the north. He turned to look to the south, to the edge of the island. There was no one in his line of sight. On Thanksgiving, lower Broadway was empty.

Back in the apartment, he looked at the empty plate on the counter, the knife and fork, the cranberry sauce in a bowl, the wine glass that guarded the placemat. "That's just sad," he said, shaking his head.

He ate quickly. Soon, the dishes were in the chugging washer. Leftovers were cooling before they'd be packed in the refrigerator. Now, Jack had the rest of the day to kill. He could do laundry. On the holiday, he would have every washing machine and dryer to himself. He poured another glass of wine.

And then came an email from Carpenter with two attachments: a few of his tracks; and Katy's set at the Bitter End. Unaware Jack was immune to self-promotion and negotiation, Carpenter thanked him for his visit and his willingness to listen to his tracks. "Shows what I can do." Jack felt a vague obligation to listen to A.A. Carpenter and the Black Canyon City Band. But he wanted to hear Katy now.

Jack pulled his laptop into the living room and plugged it into the TV's speakers. As he downloaded the file, he tried to recall what it was like at a Greenwich Village club back then. Many acts per night. Everyone on the bill allotted time for five or six songs. An artist with a following could go on whenever he chose: last, in order to imply that he was the headliner; around 11 p.m., when the club was most crowded; or first, to load in directly onto the stage, do a set, and then move on. By the sound of the applause on the track Jack heard at Carpenter's, he figured Katy went on somewhat early, performing mostly for whoever happened into the Bleecker Street club.

He closed his eyes as "Celia Remains" began. There's Katy seated on a stool, a lone spotlight, red brick behind her, Guild D-40 in her lap, Carpenter and his Telecaster at her side. "There are five thousand love songs, five thousand loves…" she sings. Bell bottoms, long black hair. She doesn't look like Susanna Hoffs or Judy Collins or Morticia Adams. She looks like Katy Emerson, fighting for her place, singing her song, showing us what she's got, who she is, and what she can do.

Jack leaned in, elbows on thighs, to listen carefully.

After "Celia Remains," Katy and Carpenter went into "Secrets of a Shy Girl." Katy fingerpicked a repeated pattern on the low strings and sang a tale of a woman longing for a familiar lover, perhaps her first lover. "I just passed the side road where we made our own rules / Where you became my lover when we were still in school." Carpenter played without intruding, sustaining notes whose volume he controlled with a pedal. The song concluded with haunting lines: "I can feel the morning on these warm and dampened sheets / It's another scarlet sunrise and you are not with me." The modest applause fell short of proper appreciation for an excellent composition very well sung and well played.

"This is good," Jack said. "I'm liking it." He wasn't in his living room. In his early 20s, he was at the Bitter End, nursing a beer at a wobbly table, someone's knee in his back.

There was a bit of noise from the stage; the mike stand creaked as it moved. Under the audience chatter, clinking glasses, a cough or two, Jack heard footsteps: Frye boots on the boards. Then, an arpeggiated chord on the piano. Hmm, he thought, already she was a better pianist back when she made that wrong-headed arrangement of "That Didn't Last Too Long" for her demo. Nevertheless, he braced for a repeat of a substandard performance.

Instead, Katy played a rather nice, bluesy version of "Walk Away Renée," a hit for the Left Banke in 1966. Rather than adhere to the pop arrangement, her take was closer to Rickie Lee Jones' reading years later. Katy's voice was assertive yet it pulled back in order to set up the sing-a-long hook. The whole thing worked.

As the sparse applause began to fade, Jack heard a pop on the tape. Then a little bit of an electronic squeal, signaling the tape had been stopped and restarted or crudely edited. When applause returned, it was more robust than what it had following "Renée." Katy thanked the crowd. She said, "A.A. on guitar" and then introduced "Camera," clearly her closing number. The duo attacked it and Katy sang with more confidence than she had all night. On the edge of his sofa, Jack joined in the applause before silencing the file.

Odd, he thought as he unplugged his laptop. Someone had deleted a song from the recording. How bad could it have been? On that night, she had been doing better than all right.

Hot oatmeal while wearing only a T and boxers was a risk, but Jack wasn't thinking yet. As his belly warmed, he was enticed by the crooked finger of his bed. He could go back and sleep 'til noon. He could sleep until tomorrow. He was looking at the raisins plumping in his steaming bowl.

His phone buzzed again.

"Can't a man find a little peace?" he said to the empty flat.

"Jack G.? Mary Donegal, NYPD press office. Did I wake you? I wanted to leave a voicemail."

"Sergeant Donegal," he said as he pulled down the front of his T. "I thought you forgot about me."

"Forget you, Jack G.? How could we? We're digging your playlist, Pops and me. Good stuff. Ever think about becoming a rock critic?"

"If you see an opening, let me know, OK?"

"Jack G.," she said. "Katherine Emerson. Died May 31, 1977."

"That's Katy."

"Suicide, Jack. I don't see any way around it."

Jack frowned. "Not buying it. No. Hard times, maybe, but—"

"You know the human mind, Jack G.? You're a psychologist?"

"Ah, no. Not really."

"Is that a requirement to be a music critic?" she teased.

"You never read Freud on Louis Armstrong?"

Donegal chuckled. "Good one, Jack G. Look, I'm sorry to disappoint you, but what is is what is. The case is closed, Jack. You asked, I answered. There's a saying: Speculation isn't substantiation."

"Is that actually a saying?"

Donegal said, "No. I just made it up. Pretty good, huh? Anyway…sorry."

"I'm disappointed, but no, you did good."

They were silent for a moment. Then Jack said, "Hey, can I buy you lunch one of these days?"

Donegal replied, "What the hell, Jack G. I like food."

While Jack dressed, Marta returned his email. Yes, she wrote, he could come by today. Last night, as he reviewed his notes while enjoying a second glass of wine with his cranberry-and-stuffing sandwich, he sent her a copy of the Bitter End show. Jack thought he detected an undertone of contrition in her response, its subtext an acknowledgment that she had misjudged him. He replied with gratitude.

He packed what he needed into the pockets of his leather coat. Exiting the building, he found a parade of Black Friday shoppers crowding Broadway on its way to Century 21. Jack shuffled in place until he found a lane and then hurried across to the R train.

Below ground, he swiped in. A train arrived on the Brooklyn-bound side of the platform. Passengers in puffy coats and toques exited in a rush. As maps were unfolded, he heard German, French, and an Australian accent. Where exactly was the World Trade Center Memorial? And the Wall Street bull? Jack was willing to help. But the tourists moved on as the Brooklyn-bound train pulled away.

An uptown R train wheezed into the station.

Marta Pacheco's 41st floor apartment was immaculate, everything in its right place, and appointed in light woods and florals, wall-to-wall carpeting covered here and there by Persian rugs. As she took his coat to a nearby closet, Jack stole a glimpse of the postcard view of Broadway, brake lights flashing, crowds streaming east, west, uptown, and down. A cloud passed by the window. Marta's silver-gray cat wrapped around his ankle.

"Shoo," said Marta, returning. She wore a knee-length violet-and-navy dress, belted in black, with matching shoes and several rings. A crucifix dangled on a gold necklace.

"What's her name?" Jack asked.

"Felix."

"Oh, the cat," he said. "Felix the Cat. Clever."

"It was my father's name," she replied without smiling.

Marta gestured for Jack to enter the dining room, where coffee and cookies awaited. There was a time-worn shoebox on the table, too.

"Earth Shoes," said Jack as he sat. "Fantastic. I haven't seen those in I don't know how long."

He was going to ask if they had been Katy's, but he couldn't see Marta succumbing to hippie fashion trends four decades ago.

"Coffee?" She held up the carafe.

"Please."

Jack waited until Marta was seated, black coffee at hand.

"Did you listen to the music I sent?"

She shook her head. "My relationship with Katy, it had nothing to do with her musical career. I encouraged her. Of course, I did. But it was not my world. I had graduated from New York University, I was in law school and volunteering at Doctors without Borders," she said. "I had my purpose."

"You came from Cuba?"

She nodded. "My father was a businessman, my mother a secretary."

"Did they know about you and Katy?"

Marta looked away. "They understood that Katy was my roommate."

"Where did you meet?"

For the first time, Marta brightened a bit. "At a bar in the Village. I was alone. I saw her. She was alone, too."

"I'm assuming this was a gay bar—"

"It was. We wanted to have a relationship. Both of us. But I don't think we expected much."

"You fell in love," Jack led.

"We fell in love."

"When was this?"

"July 1973."

"Katy was twenty."

"And I was about to turn twenty-four," she said.

"You robbed the cradle, Marta," he teased.

She nodded amicably. Sentiment was beginning to overtake her caution. "But equals. We were two people who liked to be in charge. We were not very passive."

"You argued?"

"Not Katy. It was always the same. I would shout and break a dish or kick the furniture—and she'd stare at me. Oh, that stare…then we would be together again."

"Carpenter said Katy was a homebody. That she might've been better off with a nice little house in New Jersey."

Marta twitched in annoyance. "No," she replied. "Katy was exactly where she wanted to be. Let me tell you something: Alan says he was Katy's friend. He was not."

"He said Katy was depressed when she returned from Nashville." Jack flipped through his notebook. He read: "'When she came back from Nashville, she was a mess. I used to say Katy went to Nashville, but Katy never came back.'"

Marta shook her head in disgust. "When Katy came back from Nashville, she was furious. Not depressed. Furious. And more determined."

"Why?"

"I don't know exactly. Remember, by then, we were not together."

"Because she left for Nashville?"

Marta said, "No. We were going our separate ways. I had to grow up. Our fantasy, it could not be sustained. Even if she stayed in New York, we were at our end."

Jack wrote slowly. Back then, Marta was heading deeper into the straight corporate world. An open relationship with a gay musician was in conflict with the image she might've needed to convey. At the same time, Katy was onto her new thing, whatever it was going to be.

"Where was she living when she came back?"

"With musicians she knew? I don't know. I don't think she was here for more than a few weeks when she died."

"Did Katy ever explain why she went to Nashville?"

"That is a question for Alan."

"He encouraged her to try Nashville?"

Marta nodded.

Jack frowned. "Why would he do that? I can't see any indication that she could cut it there, not right away. And she wasn't doing bad here. If you listen to that Bitter End show, Marta, there's a lot of promise there. She could've kept gigging in the Village until someone showed an interest." Jack sipped his hot coffee. "Did Carpenter know Nashville? Did he work there?"

"He said he had." She tamped the lace tablecloth. "I tell you this about Alan: If you think he will help you find Katy, you are making a mistake. Alan is for Alan."

Jack thought of Carpenter's tracks he hadn't yet listened to.

"About Katy's death," he said, "was there ever a thought that it might not have been suicide?"

"No one knows."

"What do you think, Marta?"

"I don't know. We had one conversation, very brief. We ran into each other. University Place. A Spring day, I remember. Like I said, she was furious. She said Nashville was a mistake. What were her words? It's full of 'sharks'? 'Snakes'? But she didn't want to confide in me. And maybe I didn't want to know too much." Her eyes drifted. "She was complex. She always knew how to keep to herself."

As Jack wrote, she added, "After a minute, we stood in silence. I don't think either of us said goodbye. Both of us, we walked away. If Katy hadn't died, it would've been just two people who loved each other but had to move on."

"When the police spoke to you, Marta, had they already made up their minds?"

"The interview was perfunctory. If you ask me if they were confirming a theory, I will say yes."

"Marta, what do you think happened?"

She stared across the table. "I don't know if fury ever leads to despair. Does it? I saw her as willing to fight those snakes. But I always did think the best of her. I told you. She would never surrender. And isn't suicide an act of surrender?"

He shrugged.

"I spoke to the police," Marta said, "but I never heard another word about her death. Until you."

Jack reached into the back of his notebook and removed the Lone Star Café coaster. He passed it across the table.

"Katy had this with her on the night she died. The area code is in Nashville."

Marta studied it and shook her head.

"I called," Jack said. "It's an animal shelter now. It opened in the late 1990s."

Marta returned the coaster.

"I will admit that I could have been more patient. I regret it now. When I suggested she go back to school, she said no. 'I am a musician. I write songs,' she said. I told her, 'Katy, right now you are a waitress.' You can imagine how she reacted to that."

"I didn't know she was a waitress."

"Yes. At the Lone Star," Marta said, nodding toward the coaster. "To be near the music, I suppose."

Jack told her that Katy also had a matchbook from the club in her purse when she died.

"Like I said, I didn't know that world. And I never wanted to."

While Marta refilled his cup, Jack organized what he had learned. Marta, who had studied law, thought the cops had tried to make what little evidence they had fit a scenario in which a depressed singer-songwriter killed herself. And untrustworthy A.A. Carpenter nudged Katy toward Nashville. Why? To what end?

Jack said, "Let's look at those photos. OK?"

Marta opened the box. "Oh," she said, "I should have remembered this for you."

She removed two cassette tapes and passed them over to Jack.

He said, "Is that Katy's handwriting?" One read: "The Bitter End, July 1974."

"It is," Marta replied.

"I wonder if this is the same show Carpenter sent me."

"You can take them," she told him. "I have never listened to them. I never will."

"Why not?" Jack asked sincerely, as he put the tape on top of his notebook.

Marta stood. "I can still hear her voice. She thought I wasn't listening… But no, I prefer to remember when she was singing only for me."

She dug into the box, rooted around a bit and withdrew several little spiral memo pads.

"We used those in elementary school," Jack said, as she handed them to him.

"I see girls now with their iPhones tucked in their back pockets," she said as she continued to rummage. "Katy used to keep one of those like that at all times. We would be walking along, talking, and suddenly she would stop, pull it out of her pocket and make some notes."

"Lyrics."

"And ideas. Strategies. 'Katy, you're not listening to me,'" I would say."

"The subconscious mind asserts itself."

She gathered a few Polaroids.

"That girl was always writing, always thinking. Planning ahead."

Now Marta handed Jack his coat. He tucked the photos and memo pads she'd given him into his notebook. As Felix watched, he dipped into a side pocket. He withdrew a small ball of tissue paper and handed it to Marta. "Careful," he warned.

Marta opened the tissue and saw the turquoise earrings Jack had found among Katy's belongings.

"I think Katy would want you to have them," he said.

Marta gasped. "We bought these for each other. We had nothing, and we bought these to share."

He put the cassette tapes inside his coat. "Be happy, Marta," Jack said.

Chapter Nine

Polaroids covered the ottoman. Jack had rearranged them in what he considered chronological order: Katy Shayne, tall, bony knees in a short skirt, smiling sheepishly as she opened a wrapped gift, no doubt from Marta. In wide-bottomed bells and a crocheted vest, Katy at a turntable and receiver at a house party—same apartment as in the previous photos: the one she shared with Marta? A real '70s Village vibe with spider plants in macramé plant hangers, a dream catcher, beaded door curtain. Patchouli oil in the air, a faint trace of pot? Herbal Essence shampoo in the shower caddy? "Katy, step aside," said Jack, who wanted to see what album was spinning. A third photo in the apartment: Katy on the sofa, the long fingers of her left hand forming a G chord on her Guild guitar, multi-tipped pen in her right hand as she jotted in her little notebook, frowning in concentration, hair tucked behind her ears.

Jack found her appealing in that natural, languid way girls projected way back then. A healthy hippie, already self-aware. A young woman at ease, at least when Marta held the camera. Focused as she worked on her song. Coming into a club, guitar case at her side, determination rising, Katy would've made an impression. The audience perks up when she climbs on stage and approaches the mike. Then her talent takes over.

More photos: Katy in winter in Washington Square Park. Chilly, but no snow on the ground. Framed by the Memorial Arch, arms wide like George Harrison in the "Help!" logo. Big smile and, look, her Earth Shoes. Happy woman. He lifted the photo. Katy was wearing the tortoise earrings she shared with Marta. Happy woman in love.

Then Nashville. And then dead.

He looked at the photo.

"You found a home here, Katy. And love. You showed promise. Why risk it in Tennessee?"

He walked to the kitchen counter and retrieved the cassette Marta had given him In Katy's script: "The Bitter End, July 1974."

Jack opened the plastic case. Inside, she had written the setlist. It began with "Celia Remains," then on to "Secrets of a Shy Girl," and so forth.

But this one included the song that had been clipped from the version of the show Carpenter had forwarded to him. "That Didn't Last Too Long."

Jack remembered it from the demos. Katy had played in on piano. It hadn't worked with that kind of arrangement. But if it wasn't suitable for performance, why did she keep playing it? Katy was willful, but would she drag down a show by insisting a sub-par number be included?

He tried to remember if there was a cassette player in the apartment. Eager to resume, he didn't want to wait to return to Associated Music and have it converted to files.

He looked toward a carton Molly had stored on a shelf above the coat closet. Gingerly climbing the footstool, stretching with care, he retrieved the box. It was filled with flashlights, batteries, candles and stick matches—an emergency kit in case of a blackout. Also, a brick-sized clock radio with a built-in cassette player.

"Katy," he said as he climbed down, "once upon a time, I had the best stereo system. Panasonic Technics receiver and Direct Drive turntable. Speakers with a woofer the size of your head. Dual cassette deck. Totally boss. Now look at me..."

Jack ran a dish towel around the brick to wipe away the dust, then installed batteries he had stashed in the freezer. Immediately, the radio began to hiss.

He snapped the tape onto the sprockets and pressed the proper button.

Within seconds, he knew he was hearing the same show that Carpenter had sent.

He fast-forwarded the tape past "Celia Remains," "Secrets of a Shy Girl," and most of the solo piano version of "Walk Away, Renee." As he listened to the applause following that last number, he expected Katy to play her way on piano into "That Didn't Last Too Long." But no. He heard her walk across the stage and pick up her guitar. The microphone stand creaked as she resettled on her stool.

"Ready?" she said to Carpenter. "One, two…"

Jack heard the two guitars chug E chords. Katy had rearranged her composition. Now, it had the same sort of light country-rock vibe as the Eagles' version of "Peaceful Easy Feeling."

Katy sang, "Just the other night, I was thinking of you / Isn't it amazing what a little thought can do?"

Jack listened to the song unfold. Carpenter altered his attack as the duo went to the G# bridge and it added to the surprise of the unexpected chord. The stop-start after the bridge was a nice touch. Soon, they brought the performance to its end, with Carpenter adding a little filigree as the last E chord faded. The audience applauded in appreciation, and why not? Jack thought it was the best thing Katy played that night.

"Nice, Katy, nice," he said.

He stopped the tape. In the sudden silence, he said, "But I know that song, that arrangement. I've heard it before. Where?"

Drumming his fingers on the counter, he tried to focus but could only get so far. He paced, trying to shake free a distant memory.

Whenever he thought he was edging closer to remembering a similar song he had heard years ago, "Peaceful Easy Feeling" popped into his head.

Pacing. "Yeah, I know that song…" Pacing. "Where have I heard it sung before?" Pacing. "A man cut it. A country kind of guy. Not a hit. An album track. Who?"

He couldn't place it. Jack, who could recite lyrics from songs he hadn't heard in 30 years. Jack, who could cite liner notes as if they were Scripture.

He flipped through his file cabinet brain but couldn't locate the recorded version of "That Didn't Last Too Long." Age 65, he thought; files gone missing? They say that's a thing.

He heard fiddles, but with a rock rhythm section; the track was on the country side of the line, but the singer-songwriter thing was nearby.

Naturally, Jack went to the artists in the Eagles' circle of pals, but in their music, there was none of the hardcore country elements he heard in the version he couldn't place: the twang in the singer's voice, the chicken-plucking on the Baja Telecaster, the subtle application of a mandolin deep in the mix. Not yet the full Garth Brooks kind of production, though. More mid-1970s. Eddie Rabbit, kind of, a little bit of folkabilly.

"Arggh," said Jack in frustration. He clenched his fists.

He ate cereal for dinner and drank the lukewarm milk at the bottom of his bowl. Over on the ottoman, the Polaroids were as he had left them. As he stepped down from the stool, he noticed Katy's little spiral memo pads on Molly's side of the sofa.

The green one still wore a price sticker: 29¢.

Jack sat and began to thumb through.

"You can't go back, you cannot run away / You can't renege on the statement you gave," Katy had written in ink. "You made a promise you can't undo." No girly curlicues like in her teen journal. Here, bold, stabbing letters filled up the page.

"Wake up and turn on the light / Put an end to the dead and the night" was written on the next page. Same ink. Same song?

A page later. Hmmm. She hadn't learned how to notate music. She had the chords, but described the riff as "open G, G up an octave on the B string, E to D on the G string, to C, etc." She added: "Don't slide. Pick each note."

Then: "Bass? Toms with mallets?"

Meaning she wrote it with a band in mind.

Katy the Folk Singer was moving on, just as she said she would when she was still a kid.

Sure enough, on the next page a drawing that was more than a doodle. Five stick figures, one holding drumsticks, two holding guitars, one a bass. And a self-portrait downstage at the mike.

"You were no artist, Katy, but this is kind of adorable…"

Red ink. "Don't forget to say you will always understand / We are Born Outsiders."

Blue ink. "I don't want to be out there where they fight / I just wanna be with her tonight / I'm looking for the girl / Somebody to love / I'm looking for the girl."

Whoa. Were you really going to, Katy? A five-piece band with an out lead singer?

Red ink: "Then there's this light coming down from some overhead crack in the day."

Next, Katy was musing about band names.

"The Tigers." She let that one stand.

She considered "Hour Glass," then crossed it out.

Then: "Pumpkin pound cake for Marta's bday."

Jack said, "Ladies and gentlemen, please welcome—Pumpkin Pound Cake!"

Red ink again. Days later? "Big Six" followed by a question mark. (Not a great name for a quintet.)

"Petaluma." Also crossed out. Almost works, thought Jack. But what do I know? He'd thought "Wings" was a dumb name for McCartney's post-Beatles band.

Next page: Emmylou Harris and the Hot Band. Linda Ronstadt and the Stone Poneys. Rick Nelson & the Stone Canyon Band.

Katy Shayne and the Black Canyon City Band.

Jack walked to his office. Opening his laptop, he clicked on the file Carpenter had sent.

The one he labeled A.A. Carpenter and the Black Canyon City Band.

The opening track was titled "You Can't Go Back."

The third: "Born Outsider."

Fourth: "Looking for the Girl."

Behind the counter at Eldridge Guitars, A.A. Carpenter faced a long rack of used Gibsons and Fenders hanging by their headstocks. Wearing a flannel shirt with a hole in the pocket, the triple XL guitarist had an egg sandwich in hand and a sliver of yolk in his beard.

Jack entered smiling, so Carpenter smiled, too.

"Did you listen?" He put down his breakfast.

"I did," said Jack as he unzipped his leather coat. His notebook was in his pocket. "The Black Canyon City EP?"

Carpenter said, "What did you think?"

"You hired the right players. Straddled country and rock. Where did you cut it?"

"Fort Payne, Alabama."

"Home of the band Alabama. That explains the cover, 'Fire on Fire.' Teddy Gentry wrote it. Am I right?"

Carpenter took a bite from the sandwich. "He did. Those guys I hired? They played with Alabama."

"The other tracks?"

"They're mine."

"No, they're not," Jack said. "They're Katy's."

Carpenter stumbled. "She had a hand in them, sure, but she only had a few sketches. We talked about them a whole bunch."

"Not sketches. I can recognize her use of language, her rhymes, phrasing."

Carpenter amended quickly. "I mean, I fleshed them out and wrote the music. Did the arrangements."

"Doesn't add up. There's no history of collaboration with Katy. She wrote her own music—"

"Not for a full band."

"—and she wrote the riff for 'You Can't Go Back.' She was planning a band she was going to call Black Canyon City."

"*We* were planning."

"Where's Black Canyon City?"

He shrugged. "It's just a name."

"Arizona. Her maternal grandfather lived there. I've got her notes. You're not in them. Not a single mention. Did you register the songs with BMI or ASCAP?"

"Of course."

"Under your name, maybe. Not hers." Jack had his phone in his hand. He waved it, indicating he had made his calls. "Her brother, who manages her copyrights, never heard of these songs."

Carpenter leaned toward Jack. "Listen, if I sell my record, she'll get her credit." He took up a paper napkin to wipe his hands. "I told her I was going to cut a bunch of songs for my album, hers included."

"She died in 1977, but you told her you were going to cover an Alabama song copyrighted almost twenty years later?"

"I didn't cut them all at the same session."

"No? Same room. Same air. Same setup on the drums. I wouldn't be surprised if you cut them all in one or two days."

Outside, an Entenmann's delivery truck was clogging Eldridge Street. A toddler bundled in his stroller pointed enthusiastically at the driver and his cake-laden dolly.

"I told you. If I sell that—"

"Why did you delete "That Didn't Last Too Long" from the Bitter End tape?"

Carpenter answered quickly. "Because I played like shit."

"No," said Jack. "I've heard the whole set. That was your best number."

"What do you want me to say? I didn't like nothing about it."

"Oh please," Jack said, shaking his head in disgust. "You know you nailed it on that tune. There's a reason you cut it—"

"I didn't edit the tape. All right?" Carpenter retreated, his back all but touching a wall of cables and sets of guitar strings. "That's how he gave it back to me."

"Who?"

"I told you. I had nothing to do with it."

"'It'? What's 'it'?"

Carpenter stuffed his sandwich in the trash and wiped down the counter with his sleeve. "I've got to go to work…"

"Why did you send Katy to Nashville? She wasn't ready yet. You knew it."

"I didn't send anybody nowhere. She split with Marta and wanted a change. I said, 'Try Nashville.' That's it."

"And she just hopped on a bus? That's not Katy," Jack said. "And you weren't going with her. So much for your joint Black Canyon City Band."

"I might've caught up. I had a few things going here and there."

"Bullshit," Jack said. "You stole her plan. It took you decades to do something with it."

Carpenter fidgeted with a stack of glossy trade magazines.

"Tell me what happened to her."

"No, I don't think I will," Carpenter said. Passing the cash register, he came around the counter toward Jack, towering over him. "I'm thinking you need my help."

"Is that so?"

"You won't find out how the song got to Grady by yourself."

Jack jolted. Grady. Grady Tell. That's it. Only Tell didn't call it "That Didn't Last Too Long." His version was titled "Our Love Will Never Be Gone." It was the B side of his lone hit, "Sunday Nights and Monday Mornings."

"You gave the tape to somebody down in Nashville, and Grady Tell made off with her song," Jack said. "Did Katy know?"

"Katy found out. Sure she did."

"But you didn't tell her."

Carpenter shook his head.

"You sent her into the trap."

"What trap? Nothing was happening here for her. I thought she could cut it once she got there. He would back her."

"Who's 'he'?"

"Not if you're going to write that I didn't credit Katy when I cut my tracks?"

"We'll see." Carpenter could spin it: He hadn't earned from Katy's compositions. She might've needed a hand arranging her songs for a full band. If accused, he could claim he recorded the songs in tribute to Katy and mismanaged the copyrights. "Give me the name."

"Fuck me," Carpenter moaned. "Victor Loew. All right?"

Jack took out his notebook. "Never heard of him."

"You wouldn't have. He was a song plugger, mostly. Not a top guy."

"But he had a B side on a big hit. Money, in other words."

"I didn't know he was going to cut her out completely," Carpenter insisted. "Man, you got to know producers have been stealing credit forever. Katy wasn't dumb. She figured out the game down there."

Jack stared at Carpenter. There was nothing in Katy's history to suggest she would let anyone rip off her song and hijack her career. Katy Shayne did not retreat or compromise.

The door to the shop opened, and in walked a man and a young teen. Father and daughter. Muting their enthusiasm, they took off their stocking hats in unison and shook off the cold.

Carpenter pointed to the customers as they headed toward new guitars, amps, pedals, and such. "You got it now. Victor Loew. And his son Vic," he said. "And keep me the hell out of it."

"Not if you tip him off," Jack warned.

Carpenter turned to catch up with his potential customers.

Jack hailed a cab. An SUV pulled up. He climbed inside, took out his phone, opened the AllMusic app and looked up Grady Tell. Jack had heard "Sunday Nights and Monday Mornings" many times, mostly in passing. A tale of a man who couldn't wait for sunrise after a desperately lonely Sunday, it was second-rate Kristofferson with none of his insight, word play or the stubborn weariness that came across in his melodies and vocals.

According to AllMusic, Tell released three albums and, after his death, the obligatory "Best of." Victor Loew and Grady Tell were cited as the composers of "Our Love Will Never Be Gone." There was no mention of Katy Shayne.

Loew was listed as the album's producer. Given he was a song plugger—a sort of an intermediary between composers and publishers—Jack figured he relied heavily on the studio's engineers to get the best out of Tell for his "Sunday Nights and Monday Mornings" album. In the credits, were a group of Nashville musicians Jack had come to appreciate over the years. Loew hiring top talent told Jack he knew the title track had breakout potential. And maybe Katy's song did too.

On Chambers Street, Jack paid the driver and scooted into the building. In the warmth of his apartment, Jack hung up his coat, washed his hands in the kitchen sink and entered his office.

He found "Sunday Nights and Monday Mornings" on Spotify. The title track has been streamed about five million times, and "Our Love Will Never

Be Gone" about 45,000 times.

He clicked on the "play" arrow.

Tell's "Our Love Will Never Be Gone" kicked off like a straight country version of "Peaceful Easy Feeling" with a fiddle soaring above the chugging guitars and the backbeat. Jack noted that Tell had transposed the key to D—perhaps not coincidentally, the key in which the Eagles played their tune—and the singer entered low from below with a touch of Conway Twitty in his rumbling baritone.

The opening lines had been changed. Now it was: "On a warm and lonely night, I was thinking of you / You were walking through the moonlight shining in our room." That bit of clunk hardly gave Loew and Tell the right to erase Katy.

The studio pros teed up the F# bridge beautifully and the fiddler played a long, looping line as the guitarist issued a nifty filigree. Jack nodded in approval. It was a very pleasing performance. If only Katy Shayne had been the singer.

A track like that would've made a lot of people in the industry pay attention to her. Might've given her a leg up on a satisfying and perhaps lucrative career.

Might've made her dreams come true.

Working couldn't keep Jack from the long weekend blues.

He was missing Molly: her life force, her sense of purpose, her many dimensions, her appreciation of things great and small, her glow. Life was better, and the world seemed in proper order, when one of the world's best people was nearby.

From his seat on the sofa, he turned toward the empty kitchen. His 65-year-old back tugged at him as he stood. Flexing his wrists, he returned to his office and sat at his screen.

There, in last summer's edition of *Tennessee Magazine*, was a feature about Victor Loew, a resident at the Rolling Meadows Terrace, a senior living community in Oak Hill. Now 87, Loew was once the youngest song plugger; he was 16 when he began stalking publishers in Nashville. Now, he was the oldest survivor of the pre-Music Row days.

There were photos of Loew, then and today. Way back when, he was a fit, robust young man in casual clothes: a light blazer with broad shoulders, a checked shirt buttoned to the collar, his smile projecting confidence and maturity. More than a half-century later, Loew looked like Rich Uncle Pennybags, the plump man with the white mustache in the Monopoly game. For the recent magazine photo, he wore a dress shirt, tie and suit, the slacks high above his waist. Seated in stippled sunlight on a bench outside the Rolling Meadows Terrace, his arm outstretched along the top of its back plank. Victor Loew seemed at least 20 years younger. Under the mustache, he still had a blast of a smile.

Loew came to Nashville from, of all places, the Bronx. He dropped out of Columbia and headed south. "I was a music prodigy. I understood it inside out and upside down," he told the magazine. He arrived in Nashville after World War II. "America was heading in a new direction. The war pushed people together from all over. Planes, trains, the interstate. I heard Eddy Arnold, and I knew the music would travel national. Guys here could write a damned fine song and play the heck out of it."

Coming to Nashville and sweeping floors at WSM, the radio home of the Grand Ole Opry, taught him the ins and outs of the country music business. "Starting at the bottom was a blessing," he said. "I got to learn a little bit about a lot."

Loew finagled his way into a job at Acuff-Rose Music, a highly reputable music publishing powerhouse. He claimed to be in the office when Hank Williams came in, sat down and, to prove his merit, quickly wrote, "I Can't Help It (If I'm Still in Love with You)." Loew said he persuaded Fred Rose to sign him. "Coming out of New York, I had a different way of looking at things. I knew that song could be a pop hit. Man, did it have legs!"

Did a veteran industry leader like Rose need a New York kid to tell him whether Williams was handing him a great song?

The article was littered with the old man's vanity, but it was predictable boasting. He cherished the recognition. He'd had a rich life. He remained in and around Nashville; now a widower, he had been married for 43 years to a nurse from Huntsville, Alabama. Their son Victor Jr. worked in the recording industry as an engineer. Loew said his mother lived to be 102.

Wandering toward the kitchen, Jack Googled the number for the Rolling Meadow Terrace in Oak Hill. He placed the call.

"Is it possible to speak with Victor Loew?" he asked.

Whoever answered asked for his name, which Jack supplied.

"Can I have a number so Mr. Loew can return your call?"

"Well," Jack said, "I'm in New York. Maybe it's best if I call back. What's a good time?"

"Early morning is best."

Jack thanked her and rang off.

There it was. Mr. Loew, age 87, hadn't died since the profile appeared.

Chapter Ten

Jack rolled onto Molly's side of the bed before dropping his feet to the floor. His back whined in complaint, but only mildly. He peered out of the window. It had snowed lightly overnight. The sidewalks were wet and the old snow mounds were refreshed by a new coating.

He dressed and packed a bag.

"Katy, listen," he said, as he gathered his laptop. "Am I right? There's no way you would've gone along with it after Loew stole your song. But you went to Nashville just the same. Either you didn't know about Grady Tell when you left, or you were going down there to set things straight.

"Tell me. Which?"

Jack stuffed the cables for his laptop and phone into his computer bag.

"You arrived and it flew off the rails right away, didn't it?

"They set you up. Nashville is a different kind of away game, even for a woman who's been knocking around the Village scene.

"And when you came back, you were furious. You told Marta Nashville was a mistake, a snake pit.

"You weren't the type to simmer and then let it go.

"What happened, Katy, when you found out you'd been played?"

Jack scanned the apartment, making sure he'd packed all he needed.

Then he lit out for Music City.

When was the last time Jack was in Nashville?

Some Americana Music Association thing. Jeff Tweedy, a worthy honoree. The next day, he stopped by the McCrary Sisters' home to say hello. When the conversation ended, they held hands and prayed, insisting Jack join the circle. He had never engaged in that kind of thing before.

In his rented Subaru SUV, he now breezed into the Holland Tunnel, and soon he was on the high ramp up to the New Jersey Turnpike. Moments later, downtown Manhattan was in view, as was the Statue of Liberty in the harbor.

He drove on in silence, lost in a maze of thoughts.

He imagined Katy on a bus out of New York to Nashville, her guitar and suitcase in the overhead rack, surrendering her place in New York for… What? Was there anything about Katy Shayne to suggest she was impulsive? That she moved on without a plan? No. She got on that bus with a level of confidence. Carpenter told her Victor Loew was waiting—Victor Loew, who knew Hank Williams, Fred Rose and Music Row. Katy knew she was good and getting better. With folk dead in the Village, she saw a new path toward her goal.

"You know it sounds so easy on the TV or at a show / But when it comes so easy, you never know," sang Katy on the bridge to "That Didn't Last Too Long." Sang Grady Tell in "Our Love Will Never Be Gone."

It never came easy for Katy, Jack knew. She had earned what little she had gotten. She took on the challenge of Greenwich Village, and then she went to Nashville for an entirely different trial.

On the basis of one song? Without some guarantees?

The move couldn't have been made on the basis of a single song. Knocking around the New York scene, Katy would've known that the music business didn't work that way. Country songwriters compose scores of tunes in the hope of selling one.

Someone must have told Katy she could make it as a country-rock performer. Someone other than just Carpenter.

Had to be someone with a resume like Loew's.

As Jack drove past Newark Airport, roaring planes all but skimming the roof of the rental car, he reflected on Nashville in the mid-'70s. The city was abundant with great women singers. They easily could adapt to rock's rhythmic accents and instrumentation as the new hybrid emerged. Yet Katy had been convinced to try Nashville. "We're looking for women who have a taste for country, but are rooted in folk and rock," someone like Victor Loew might've told her. "Let's get you into a studio and see what catches fire. Hell, Ronstadt is from Tucson, Bonnie Raitt from Burbank, John Fogerty from Berkeley. Just say you're from rural Jersey. Farm country. It'll play."

Having written one country-rock tune and having shown a gift for reinterpreting hits by pop composers, Katy might have been open to the idea that she had the raw stuff for the transition. She was 24 when she died. No matter how Hopewell and the Village had calloused her, she was still a kid. On her own, without Marta, she might have thought a major change was what she needed.

She had a look, too. She was naturally defiant and could easily affect a sexy sneer. With her Crystal Gayle mane, a fringe jacket, spray-on jeans and a pair of Sam Lucchese's cowboy boots, and there it is: Katy Shayne, Country Rock's new sensation.

Jack decided to pull into the next rest stop on the turnpike. He wanted coffee, maybe a scone. He found a spot near the dog walk and, stepping down gently, walked toward a building that looked like it had been made out of Lincoln Logs. The snow, heavier south of Manhattan, had been shoveled, leaving a lane of slush on the concrete. Jack navigated it carefully.

The building beckoned with the scent of cinnamon and broiling burgers. He held back the glass door, allowing a family to pass. In their church clothes, Mom, Dad and Grandma thanked him as the kids raced ahead.

He spent nights in Winchester, Virginia, and Johnson City, Tennessee, staying in the same chain hotel: free breakfast of rubbery pancakes, crumbles of dried powdered eggs, little packets of dusty oatmeal. He took apples, bananas and coffee to the Subaru. He was an efficient traveler.

He was thinking about Molly. On the road for *The Observer*, he always felt her absence when he settled into Somewhere U.S.A. He would speak as if she were in the empty hotel room. Now, as he pepped along the highway, he was thinking she would approve of his mission. He was no longer slumming at the gates of the graveyard, waiting for a rocker to die. He was making something happen. Molly was a fan of initiative and a life-long believer that good luck was self-generated.

Soon, a sun shower welcomed him to Route 40. He put his hand out to feel the gentle rain. Jack was hungry and he wanted a little roadhouse where locals sleep-walked to lunch hour. He had interviewed Townes Van Zandt in a musty place called Mom's somewhere between Austin and San Antonio—creaky wooden floorboards, wobbly chairs, every man but Jack under a cowboy hat. Townes told him the Salisbury steak needed gravy, and he was right.

Instead, he crossed a bridge and found a Chinese restaurant in a mall anchored by a Wal-Mart. He ordered takeout, then picked up extra socks, underwear and a makeshift shaving kit.

Chomping on his last dumpling, Jack arrived in Goodlettsville, on the northern outskirts of Nashville, and chose a hotel fairly close to Blunderbuss Recording Studios. It was a little too early to check in, the hotel desk clerk told him, despite his super-duper status.

"That's OK," Jack told the clerk. He returned to the parking lot and drove to a little park near muddy Mansker Creek. It was 52 degrees with little humidity. Standing in a stream of sunlight, his denim shirt unbuttoned, faded Blondie T in view, he sighed happily. The pale blue sky over central Tennessee went on forever; the scent of cedar spiced the air and pinecones dotted the turf.

After a call to the Metro Archives at the Nashville Public Library, he drove on and soon a rented Subaru with the New York plates was parked in front of Blunderbuss, which looked like an oversized bunker, square and squat, its outer walls painted white. One of those plastic outdoor ashtrays stood guard by the front door.

Notebook in hand, Jack entered a narrow corridor and proceeded past framed gold 45s and albums to a reception area furnished with two well-worn black-leather sofas, a coffee table covered in music magazines, and an old jukebox. An antique flintlock rifle was fixed to a wall.

He heard a woman's voice through a speaker. Peering up at a security camera, he said, "I'm looking for Vic Loew."

According to the magazine profile of his father, Victor Loew Jr. worked right here.

A buzzer rang and Jack entered yet another slim corridor where he found the receptionist seated behind a sliding-glass window much like the kind in a medical office. She was petite with red hair and big eyes; she wore an orange checkerboard top that had little pictures of young Elvis on some of the squares. Surrounded by filing cabinets, she had two laptops on her desk and an old-fashioned hour-by-hour calendar covered in script in different colored inks. A poster from a Country Music Association festival from a few years back filled a wall beneath two clocks, one for Nashville time, the other for the West Coast.

Jack introduced himself: "I'm Jack G. Fiorello. *The New National Observer.* Is Vic around?"

"Vic Loew?" She shook her head vehemently as she rolled back her chair. "He's not here anymore. Thank heavens."

"Do you know where I can find him?"

She said, "Hold on a minute."

Using the desk phone, she spoke to someone named Milton.

When she hung up, she said, "Go see Milton. I'll buzz you in."

Jack thanked her and opened a heavy, wheezing door. It was the entrance to the studio—a gorgeous, airy room with a vaulted ceiling, immaculate wood floor and streams of light through windows he hadn't seen on the outside. Jack was confused: The recording studio seemed too large for the building. He spun around; a 360-degree turn. Yes, a beautiful space. Why should he have expected less from a Music City satellite?

Two men were arranging chairs and music stands under ceiling-mounted baffling. Jack saw a Bosendorfer grand piano and a Hammond B-3 organ. A Pearl drum kit was minus its cymbals. Rings of cables were looped on the walls.

The older man, who wore a short-sleeved shirt, crossed the studio to meet his guest.

After they shook hands, Jack said, "Heck of a room."

Klinger nodded politely. "It gets it done." He had a long face and a hangdog expression. Jack thought he could be just north of age 50, meaning he was too young to have been in the business when Katy arrived in Nashville.

"Busy?" Jack asked.

"Pleased to be."

By now, the other man had ambled over. He resembled Klinger, though beefier and with cascading auburn hair. When Jack shook his hand, he said, "I'm Paul. Klinger. You're looking for Vic?"

"I'm looking for Vic."

"Vic doesn't work here anymore," Milton Klinger said. "Not for a while now."

Jack said, "I saw his name in some liner notes."

Neither Klinger replied.

"Is he still in the business?"

The elder Klinger said no.

Jack was picking up a trace of disapproval.

"Like that, huh?" Jack asked. "Your receptionist isn't a fan."

"Not many women are," Paul Klinger said. "Man's a walking asshole. Don't quote me."

Jack held up the sealed notebook.

Milton Klinger said, "Let's say he's more trouble than he's worth and let it go at that."

Jack said, "I'm going to try to talk to him. Is he going to be a problem?"

"He ain't half the tough guy he thinks he is and a peanut's got more sense."

Paul Klinger endorsed his father's opinion with a downward snap of his head.

"Any idea where I can reach him?"

Milton Klinger said, "I heard he's got a job at a bank in Mount Juliet. A security guard."

Wide-eyed, his son said, "They gave that fucker a gun?"

A tidy brick building with a drive-through window, Wilson Bank & Trust was on a grassy stretch of Highway 70 with an auto parts store nearby and a strip mall across the way. Jack parked next to a red Mustang convertible and entered the building, which was already dressed for Christmas. Carols done country style wafted overhead.

There was but one guard, so Vic Loew wasn't difficult to find. He was hard and wiry, jut-jawed with a dull expression, ruddy skin, maybe a decade younger than Jack. In a beige uniform with brown epaulets and a gold badge, Loew appeared more state trooper than bank security. A gold whistle hung beneath his name tag and he carried a pistol on his hip. What Jack knew about guns could fill a thimble. He had never fired one.

"Mr. Loew," he began. He introduced himself, adding *The Observer* and his title. "I'd like to talk to you about your dad."

"I'm working," said Loew, who stood against a wall by the door, his hands dangling at his sides.

"Can we set up a time?"

Vic Loew told Jack to wait. He was due a cigarette break. He walked over to a teller, said something or other, and she nodded. It seemed to Jack that Loew had asked for permission.

Jack followed him outside. There were benches around the side of the brick building. Loew headed for a slice of shade. Jack saw cars rush around a Pepsi truck out on the highway.

Loew took off his beige campaign hat to mop his forehead. He had thinning hair that he realigned with a swipe of his palm. Before they sat, Jack asked if Loew wanted to grab a late lunch. Loew said no, he needed to get back. "The money don't watch itself," he said.

"I read about your father," Jack said as they settled in. "I'm doing a story that kind of involves when country rock came to Nashville."

"'Kind of'?"

"You never know where these things will go. But your dad was there. He had the vision that Nashville didn't need to stick to the tried-and-true."

Loew sat hunched over his long legs, one crossed over the other, his hat on his knee. "Do you pay?"

"For what?" Jack thought he might have been re-considering the meal.

"When you interview someone. Do you pay?"

"I haven't yet," Jack replied. "Does he demand payment?"

"You'll get paid. Right?"

"Maybe. There's no story until there's a story."

Loew looked at his cigarette and let out a low groan of disinterest. He was treating the conversation as an annoyance. Jack knew how to work a source and create a natural dialogue.

He said, "I'll put it this way: Who's going to know what happened when people like your father are gone?"

"When do you want to do it?"

"Today? Tomorrow?"

"He gets upset. He's old."

"That's why I came to you first," Jack told him. "People his age, though, they seem to enjoy reminiscing. They like to know they're not forgotten."

Loew took a long final drag. He looked to toss the butt onto the concrete, but thought better of it and walked it to the ashtray atop the garbage can. When he turned, he stared at Jack, still suspicious.

"What can I tell you?" Jack said. "I'm legit." He repeated his pen name including the letter "G." "You can check it out."

"I'll ask my father. Give me your phone number."

Jack scribbled it on a back page of his notebook, then tore out the sheet.

Loew folded the paper and put it in his breast pocket.

"You came a long way."

Jack nodded.

"Kind of dumb when you could've called."

"When else am I going to get to meet an eighty-seven-year-old prodigy? It will be an honor."

With two hands, Loew put on his hat just so and ambled back toward the bank.

Jack heard the buzzing of his phone in the wobbly distance. He had fallen asleep in his clothes. Travel took its toll. As he spun to stand, he kicked his laptop off the bed. It landed with a dull thud.

His phone was across the room on the hotel desk. He bumbled toward it, careful to avoid stubbing his toe on the chair.

It wasn't Molly, as he had hoped. It was a blocked number.

"Fiorello," Jack croaked. According to the nightstand clock, it was 6:15. In the morning, said the dull light peeking through the shades.

"He'll see you today."

"Loew? That you?"

"He'll see you today," Vic Loew repeated. "Don't give him a hard time."

Jack sat on the edge of the bed. "Are you coming?"

"I've got to work. Be ready for the exact time." He cut the connection.

Jack lumbered to the bathroom. There had been less drama and subterfuge in arranging an interview with Prince at Paisley Park. Jack recorded it. Prince said 741 words. About 300 of them were about Amos Garrett's guitar in Maria Muldaur's "Midnight at the Oasis."

Returning but still dazed, Jack looked around the room. Apparently, he'd had takeout from Buffalo Wild Wings for dinner. So much for sampling the local cuisine.

He tried to remember last night. No trip to Nashville. He wasn't on a search for new talent, and the Ryman was presenting a dad-rock band Jack had seen at least a half-dozen times and never really enjoyed. He cleaned the rental car, tossing out banana peels, an apple core, and a copy of the *Roanoke Times*. He padded around the hotel room. He researched Music Row. If Victor Loew was a player, he was never more than a minor one.

Now, the morning after, Jack shook his head. He couldn't remember when he dropped off to sleep. He threw open the blinds to let in the Tennessee sunlight. He saw the outline of nearby trees, robust even on the edge of winter.

He was in the parking lot of a Waffle House halfway to Oak Hill when Vic Loew called.

"Now," said Loew with snark and melodrama.

Jack hopped into the Subaru to drive to Rolling Hill Terrace. Mid-morning traffic on Route 65 was light, even with strip malls on either side of the highway. The sky was silvery gray.

He eased off the gas and snuggled into the turn lane to make a hard left. He looked at the overhead red arrow. There were birds on the wire.

Soon, it was Jack's turn to drive on. Traffic flowed until he ran into construction on a stretch that fed toward Nashville proper. Cars inched in behind him. Up popped in his mind the gray-stone castle of Nashville's Union Station. Now a grand hotel, Jack once had an early evening drink in its lobby bar under soaring limestone arches and stained glass. He was passing time before he was off to the Ryman to see John Prine, with whom he spent an entertaining afternoon. The bartender welcomed him with warmth. After serving him, she said, "I've seen you before, haven't I?"

Jack sipped his beer. "Who can say?"

"You're on TV."

Jack had been on network television about a dozen times over the years. It was a waste of time. He was a terrible guest. He answered thoughtfully, honestly. He didn't understand how to inhabit a role. He actually was Jack, not someone playing Jack.

"I'm David Hasselhoff," he told her.

Now horns honked, and Jack realized he hadn't kept the line moving. He tapped the gas, bore left and waved a general apology. Within minutes, the Oak Hill exit came into view, and in no time, Jack was off the highway and sweeping through verdant countryside toward Rolling Meadows Terrace. Waiting for a passing van carrying medical supplies, he turned at a sign on the roadside that said the senior center was near.

Rolling Meadows Terrace had borrowed the look of a handsome, old-fashioned resort: white with green shutters, a sweeping lawn guarded by knee-high white-picket fences. He was greeted at the booth at the top of a small hill and, after a phone call up to the main building, told to drive on. He passed black-walnut trees and coasted toward a white portico from which hung the flags of the U.S. and the state of Tennessee. Parking in a visitor's spot a short walk from the entrance, Jack took up his notebook and stepped into the gray sunlight. Sixty degrees, said Jack's weather app. He left his coat on the back seat.

Jack was greeted by a gray-haired Black man who introduced himself as Mr. Reeves. A senior administrator, he said, as sliding doors whooshed open and they stepped inside the retirement center.

"You write for *The New National Observer*," said Mr. Reeves, who was in short sleeves and a tie that looped over his plump stomach.

Jack nodded.

"And you're interested in Mr. Loew."

"I am."

They passed green leather sofas set in a wide semi-circle on a red marble floor. White rocking chairs faced a large bay window that overlooked a rainbow of flowers in a garden.

"Where is everybody?" Jack asked.

"PT—physical therapy, that is. Classes. Arts & Crafts. Yoga."

"Yoga?"

He smiled. "It's voluntary."

"People pushing ninety doing yoga," Jack mused. "That's encouraging."

"Mildred Bauer is one hundred and four," he said. "She plays golf. Nine holes every day."

To Jack's left and right were long, brightly lit corridors. Extra-wide doors accommodated wheelchairs.

"Apartments?" he said, pointing with his notebook.

"On the ground floor, yes. Upstairs, you'll find a more traditional care environment. But our residents come to Rolling Meadows to be independent."

Another pair of glass doors wheezed open, and they stepped outside to a lawn cleaved by a path lined with benches identical to the one in the photo of Victor Loew that was in the magazine.

"Weeping beech," Jack said, as they passed a gnarled tree.

"They were here long before we were."

"My wife likes a good weeping beech."

Loew came into view as the path sloped downward. In a wheelchair pushed by an attendant, he wore a gray suit and bright tie, a green Rolling Meadows blanket on his lap. Jack watched as Loew held out his hand, and the attendant helped him to his feet. Slightly hunched and moving slow, he nevertheless looked as dapper as he did in the photo, his white mustache neatly combed. As Jack stepped in to shake his hand, he could see Loew was alert, robust, right there, a little cocky even.

"*The New National Observer,*" Victor Loew mused. "Read it every day. I still manage my own portfolio."

"I'm guessing you do all right," Jack said, nodding toward the center's quietly stylish main building.

"Well, I guess I do."

Loew teeter-tottered to sit. Tapping the green wooden bench with the flat of his mottled hand, he beckoned Jack to join him in the sun.

Mr. Reeves excused himself and withdrew, roly-polying up the incline. The attendant pushed the empty wheelchair across the lane. He stood facing them.

"He's Joey," said Victor Loew. "I don't mind him much."

Jack said, "Hi, Joey."

Joey nodded. In his green Rolling Meadows warm-up suit and white shoes, he locked hand-to-wrist behind his back as if on guard duty. Jack thought of Vic Loew at the Bank & Trust.

Jack tilted his head to let the sunlight stroke his face.

"You can't beat it," Loew said. "How's the weather in New York?"

"Depends if you like brutal winters. I'll take the summer."

"I haven't been to New York in forty years, I'll bet you."

Jack looked at him. "Is it something we said?"

Loew swept his hand toward the greenery, the perfect sky, the ridges in the distance.

"Yeah," Jack said, "I get it."

"And I worked until I was seventy-nine."

"Loew Publishing."

"You know about that?"

"Background. *Tennessee Magazine.* You helped build Music Row. Nice profile."

"I didn't say half the things she put in there."

A claim often heard by journalists from their subjects, even when the interview is recorded.

"You were a player."

He nodded with pride.

"Did your son tell you what I want to talk about?"

"Country rock. When the world came to Nashville. I was there."

Jack opened his notebook. "Tell me about what it was like. Plugging songs."

"You've got to know the terrain," he said, holding up his hands. "You got songwriters here, you got publishers over there. You bring them together." He locked fingers.

"There's more to it than that," Jack led.

"You've got to know who's right for it. When you walk through the door, they've got to know you're reliable."

"Who do you represent?"

"The song," Loew said.

"Meaning the composer."

"Meaning the composer. But you bring three songs in a row to a Chet Atkins, an Owen Bradley, a Don Law and they're not right, maybe the door won't open so easy when you come calling. You don't last long in this business by wasting everybody's time."

Jack continued to scribble. Note-taking in longhand was a tactic. Every now and then, the subject would fill the silence, saying more than he had intended.

"Where do you get the songs? That is, how do you discover the composers? They come to you?"

"Eventually, but when you're starting out, you hustle."

"Even though you had been with Acuff-Rose."

Loew nodded.

Without looking up from his notes, Jack said, "I'm under the impression that back in the '60s, Harlan Howard, Hank Cochran and Willie Nelson were in a booth at Tootsie's banging out three hits a day."

"They might have been," he said. "But remember, I came here right after the war. Let me tell you something. There was no here back then. The world of country music didn't have a headquarters. Sure, there was WSM downtown but—"

"Where you worked. WSM."

"Where I worked. You had the Opry at the Ryman, which was on NBC. Eddy Arnold—he was from Henderson—he brought the RCA Victor people here. Then Ernest Tubb. But Music Row? Nobody would have dreamed it."

Loew preferred to mine the distant past for generalities and well-worn tales. He fouled off comments and questions that nudged him from his own mythology.

"Granted," Jack said, "and I appreciate that you were among the builders."

Loew nodded.

"But I'm not seeing a picture of you chasing down the next Harlan Howard or Willie. I know you had to work your tail off. Am I right?"

"Do you know anyone who made it who didn't?"

"So you're at Tootsie's, you're at the studios talking to producers, people are sending you demos…"

"From all over the country."

"So after a while, it makes sense that you open your own publishing company, Morningside Publishing."

Loew said, "In the Cumberland Lodge Building. Mercury had their offices there."

"And when did you start producing?"

"That's hard to say. I produced a lot of demos on songwriters. You just sort of move into it."

"So it's a full-service shop: Find the composers, vet the songs, get them to the performers, produce the sessions. As publisher, you handled the copyrights too, no?"

Frowning in suspicion, he nodded.

Jack smiled as he looked at Loew. "I like how you make it all seem so natural. But we both know that any one of those jobs you did would have been enough for success. Plus, you and your wife were raising a family. It's not that easy."

"I didn't say it was easy—"

"No, of course not. But you were driven. Why?"

He shrugged. "I had to make a living. Like you said, I had a family."

"I'm not trying to be obtuse, Mr. Loew. But I can't see it through your eyes. I'm saying who but you who's still alive had a career like that? You're the one expert."

His vanity permitted a quip. "It wasn't torture, you know. There was a social aspect. It was a way of life."

"'A way of life,'" Jack repeated. "In the music business. Making a living." He shut his notebook. "Do you think we could get some water?"

Loew looked up at the attendant who, after hesitating, nodded and headed along the path toward the main building.

Jack turned and crossed his legs. He put his notebook on the bench, his pencil in his shirt pocket.

"Grady Tell," Jack said.

Chapter Eleven

Loew said, "Why do you want to know about Grady?"

"Not so much Grady. But what it was like to finally have a Number One hit."

"He was a good boy," Loew said. "We lost a good one."

"You were close?"

"I raised him up in this business."

"I'm sorry. I didn't know," Jack said. "Who wrote 'Sunday Nights and Monday Mornings'?"

"Grady. I helped a bit."

"I didn't know you played."

"Helped with the lyrics. It's part of the job."

"That's a heck of a tune, Mr. Loew."

"I knew the marketplace. Kristofferson was writing for Combine and they had quite a few hits on him before Fred Foster signed him to record for Monument. How's a one-man shop going to compete with that?"

By mimicking his style, Jack thought. Kristofferson had an armful of Grammys and was off to Hollywood by the time Tell cut "Sunday Nights and Monday Mornings." Loew saw an opening and leapt in.

"It still has a lot of traction," Jack said. "Five million streams on Spotify."

"That's good for about fifteen cents…"

"Can I ask you about that album? Am I wrong to think that it was a hit on its own? I mean, the single lifted it, sure. But there were a bunch of good tunes on it."

Loew nodded.

"You picked them, right?"

Giving a little scratch to the top of his head, he peered along the path to see if Joey was returning.

"I'm thinking about "Our Love Will Never Be Gone." Do you remember it? Kind of like the Eagles—which was a good model in the early '70s. It's yours and Grady's, right?"

Loew said, "We covered a Jerry Jeff Walker tune on the album, but otherwise it was Grady and me. That's right."

"You were going for a country-rock sound."

"The market was just about there."

Jack said, "Do you remember a singer-songwriter who came here from New York? Katy Shayne?"

Hesitating, Loew said, "No…"

"Maybe you remember that she died back in New York in 1977."

"I was here in 1977."

"No, I know. What can you tell me about her?"

Loew said, "I can't say I met her."

Jack dipped into his pouch in his notebook and retrieved the photo Marta had given him of Katy in Washington Square Park. "That's her."

"Pretty girl," he said hesitantly.

"The cops say she killed herself. She came here, went home and the cops say she killed herself."

"'Killed herself.' Say, that's right. Yes. I did hear about that."

"I've been working it and I'm not convinced."

Loew shifted on the bench. "Are you thinking that this was a concern of mine at the time?"

Jack said, "Please, Mr. Loew. The notebook is closed. I'm trying to do right by her. I take you at your word. You're much admired."

Loew again turned to see if Joey was about to return.

"But it could be that somebody killed her. Do you have a theory? Maybe you heard something?"

"I don't want to talk about this. You didn't tell my son anything about this."

Jack shook my head. "No, no. You're one of the good guys, Mr. Loew. I know that. I'm asking for your help."

"How? What can I tell you?"

"Give me a sense of her. You can do that."

"I can't place her."

"She wrote 'Our Love Will Never Be Gone.' She called it 'That Didn't Last Too Long.'"

"Grady and me—"

"Please," Jack said. "Maybe you promised her opportunities. The kind A.A. Carpenter suggested."

"Carpenter," he muttered. "I don't… Who?"

"He talks, Mr. Loew."

Jack turned at the sound of Joey's footsteps on the path. He said, "Did you sign her?"

"She didn't write that song," he said in protest.

"I've got recordings of her playing it in Greenwich Village well before Tell cut it. How did you come to get the credit?"

Jack reached into the notebook again. This time, he took out the Lone Star Cafe coaster and placed it on Loew's thigh. Loew lifted it to examine the phone number.

"That was the number for Morningside Publishing. You were born and raised in Morningside Heights, weren't you? Near Columbia."

"How did you get it?"

Joey arrived with two bottles of water. Jack took one and quickly placed it under the bench. But Loew shook off the offer.

"I want to go back," he said.

Appealing to vanity, Jack said, "Mr. Loew, you can give this young woman the justice she deserves."

Jack waited for a response. But deflated, exposed, suddenly fragile and very old, Loew said nothing.

He held up his arm so Joey could lift him carefully off the seat. Jack stood with Loew while the wheelchair was retrieved.

"What happened when she returned to New York, Mr. Loew?" he said. "At least tell me if you know anything about that."

"I don't want to talk to you anymore," Loew replied as he waited for the wheelchair to settle behind him.

Walking uphill toward the rental car, Jack ignored the splendor of the late-morning sun, the scent of laurel and pine, the birds' songs. He climbed into the Subaru, threw down his notebook and drove directly, determinately toward the hotel. The trip passed in no time: For much of it, Jack was thinking not about traffic, the Cumberland River overpass, the Nashville skyline, the chicken-and-waffles lunch he had intended to enjoy or a little thank-you visit to librarians at the Metro Archives near the Ryman.

He was thinking about Victor Loew, who had lived 87 years, had a wife and child, accolades from local media, verdant and tranquil surroundings, an attendant who gets him his water. Victor Loew, who still managed his own portfolio, sits in the sunlight, reminiscing about a long, satisfying life. Because he kept quiet for more than four decades about an injustice he caused.

Currying favor, Carpenter sent Loew the tape of the Bitter End gig. Loew saw the potential. He led her on, but he never signed Katy. He never workshopped her around town, setting her up with the best players and arrangers. He never paid her for the song. He stole "That Didn't Last Too Long." And when Katy returned to Morningside Publishing to protest, Loew told her there was nothing she could do about it. Grady Tell wrote it, Loew could corroborate the claim and if a gay woman from New York tried to raise any kind of holy hell, he would bury her so deep she might not ever sing a song again, certainly not in Nashville or on any of the several thousand radio stations that were starting to spin country rock across the United States.

Jack was certain that's how it happened and he was going to prove it.

Arriving at his hotel, he bought a candy bar at the vending machine and hung a Do Not Disturb sign on his door. The room had yet to be serviced; the mess reflected the chaos in his mind. He needed to write now to organize, to discover what he had learned versus what was still speculation.

Pacing the hotel room, Jack looked at Katy's photo in Washington Square Park. Such glee, yet an edge. What she could have been.

He threw back the curtains and inched open the window. Tidied the desk and tossed a Wal-Mart bag off the chair.

Where to begin? he thought as he sat. He tore the wrapper off the candy bar and bit into a nutty chunk of chocolate.

Jack scrolled back on his phone and tapped a number. BMI.

"This is Jack Fiorello. *The New National Observer*. Did we speak last week?"

Yes, she said, we did.

"I've got another one for you. I'm trying to track compositions registered to, or by, Victor Loew. L-O-E-W. This would be in the 1970s and '80s. Maybe the '90s."

Jack heard her keyboard clacking.

"Victor Loew," she said. "Yes. Let's see…thirty-two songs. On his own or with co-composers."

"Thirty-two? Is one 'Our Love Will Never Be Gone?'"

It was.

"Any chance you could email me all the titles? I can track them down from there."

She said, "I don't see the harm in that."

"Me neither," said Jack G. "Hey, you guys are great. Credit where it's due."

Call done, Jack plugged in his phone to recharge. Now he was thinking. After deciding to steal "That Didn't Last Too Long," maybe Loew milked her for more. Did Katy add a bit of country to her songs and demo them with Loew? Maybe someone remembered her, someone who worked in the Cumberland Lodge Building, or an engineer who recorded her in town.

"Katy, did you make friends down here?

"Did you showcase? Open mic night at the Bluebird Café?

"Where were you living, Katy? Did you find a partner?"

He heard a sharp knock on the door.

"No service, thanks," he shouted.

Another sharp knock.

"Hold on," Jack said as he shut the laptop.

He opened the door to find Vic Loew in his beige-and-brown uniform. Red-faced, he was taut with anger.

"I want to talk to you."

Jack stepped into the hall and let the door shut behind him.

"What did you do to my dad?"

"Point that finger elsewhere," Jack told him with surprising resolve.

He jabbed Jack's chest. When Jack slapped at his hand, Loew dropped it hard to the butt of his sidearm.

"What did you do?"

Jack glanced at the gun. "I interviewed him. Like I said I would."

"You played him."

Jack said, "I didn't have to play him. He wouldn't shut up."

"I want that notebook."

"Fuck that."

Loew fumed. "You're not writing anything, you understand me?"

Jack stepped in to close the space between them. "Too late, pal. Song stolen. Dead girl. NYPD and whoever the hell else I told. Now what?"

He stared at Jack, his long face shuddering with rage.

"What kind of man leans on an eighty-seven-year-old?" he said finally.

"What kind of eighty-seven-year-old song thief sits on a thing like this for decades?"

"There's no 'thing'—"

"Yeah, there is. What's your role in it?"

"My role? The cops know, everybody knows, she jumped off the roof. Y'all gonna say she wasn't fucked up?"

Down the corridor, near her wagon full of shampoos, soaps and towels, a woman from Housekeeping watched warily.

"For the record, Loew, Katy was solid. No one but you says otherwise. Why?"

"'Why'? Who the fuck cares?" Loew shouted. "How the hell can it matter all these years—"

"She gave up everything to come here," Jack snapped. "And she wrote that song. It was her song." He waved his hand in disgust. "Your dad ripped her off. Whether you like it or not, I'm working it and Katy is going to get the credit she deserves."

"You fuckers. You reporters. No wonder everybody thinks you're shit."

"A young woman had her work stolen and you want to think somebody else is shit? That is laughable."

He said it again. "I want that notebook."

"Like I said. Fuck that."

"You know, you may be some kind of thing in New York, but down here—"

"Save it. You've had your say, you with your sidearm and your Dudley fuckin' Do-Right hat." Jack dug into the pocket of his jeans for the keycard. "Your dad should've come clean decades ago."

Loew sputtered. "I'm not done with you."

"Get lost."

As if he had to, Loew shoved Jack with the flat of his hand. Jack stumbled, bouncing against the door as Loew stormed off.

Shaking, Jack went inside.

It took Jack a while to settle down. Another long, steamy shower didn't do it on its own. Clean but not refreshed, he headed out. He placed his duffel and laptop bag in the backseat of the rental car and drove away from the hotel. Soon, he traced the Cumberland River, which dazzled with dancing sunlight. Jack rolled down the window and took in the air. As pleasing as it was, it did little to clear his jumble of thoughts.

Soon, he was toodling along a winding two-way street with one-family homes on either side, American flags limp in the lazy breeze, grass at ease. A postman whistled as he walked along, bundles of mail tucked under his arm. Jack saw a calico cat sitting on a porch, watching the cars go by.

In the near distance was a stretch of forest. Houses began to disappear and Jack was surrounded by dense trees. Thin rays of sunlight strained through and the widening road remained bright and inviting. He took a gentle turn. On a straightaway, he accelerated with ease. All ahead was clear. He let the road direct the trip as he took in the natural beauty. A dent in the blacktop caught him by surprise.

And then Jack felt the SUV wobble and quake. Without warning, it jerked hard to the left. As it let out a piercing squeal, it crossed the yellow lines, scraped onto the shoulder and hurdled toward a patch of thick tree trunks. Crashing into a ravine, it stopped with blunt force. The airbag exploded and Jack was gone.

He came to very slowly. The sun wasn't where it had been. Everything was gauzy and in a fog. His head pounded; his face ached. When he tried to move, his left shoulder screamed, and his arm hung limp.

He was still behind the wheel, the seat belt strapped across his chest. When he tried to reach to unsnap it, he saw the middle finger of his right hand was bent at an odd, unnatural angle.

He used his thumb to undo the belt.

Door ajar, he shoved it open with his foot.

He slid to stand on the turf.

The front driver's side wheel hub was exposed. Its tire rested on its side near a tree as if it had been flung away from the vehicle. A hubcap was over there. One lug nut had settled in the muck.

The rental's back door was open.

Jesus, thought Jack, I'm going to be sick.

He shuffled slowly until he could lean against the hood.

He dabbed at his nose. Fresh blood was already beginning to cake.

Slug-slowly, Jack walked around the SUV to the passenger's side. It was unlocked. He searched for the phone and, despite the star-dotted haze before his eyes, he found it between the seat and the center armrest.

He dialed 911.

He explained. "No, I don't know where I am. Can I send you my GPS coordinates?"

He said, "I think I'm hurt. I think I may be hurt bad."

The voice asked, "Sir? Hello? Hello?"

Jack crumbled. He landed on damp earth. He was lost among the trees.

He woke up in an ambulance screaming along a highway. His middle finger had been set back in place. His left arm was in a sling. His nose had been packed with cotton. He was in pain and couldn't tell where he hurt most.

Jack cleared his throat, once, twice, again.

"Where's my laptop?" he managed. "My notebook."

Chapter Twelve

Jack spent hours in the emergency room. His shoulder was popped back in place, his broken nose was set and he took 14 stitches in a wound above his left ear that required a nurse to shave away a patch of his gray hair. No concussion, the intern said, but she thought Jack should stay overnight.

They found a bed for him. His duffel, moist and mud-stained, waited on a chair, as did his leather coat. By now, it was past nine o'clock, and the man on the other side of the curtain snored like he wanted to frighten dinosaurs. Jack was hungry but also nauseous. The painkillers caused confusion. And then a cop came.

He introduced himself as Sgt. Rhett Tackett of the Davidson County Sheriff's Office and asked Jack to describe what had happened.

Jack raised the bed to look at him. "Somebody loosened the lug nuts."

"How do you know?"

"I drove down from New York. Nine-hundred miles. No issues. Suddenly, a tire flies off?"

Blond and dark-eyed, Tackett was sturdy. He projected a sense of control. Pulling up a chair, he said, "So you come to…"

A lion's roar from the other bed interrupted the interrogation. Tackett shot a glance at the curtain.

"The back door was open and the side door too and where's my laptop and notebook?"

He nodded deliberately. "And other missing items?"

"Whatever else was in my bag. Pens, pencils, earbuds. Charger cables."

"You're going to want to fill out a form."

"What's not missing: my wallet and my phone. So what does he want when he tries to kill me? My laptop and my notes."

Tackett said, "You're a journalist."

Jack nodded. After another air-ripping snore, he said, "I'm not going to last the night with that guy."

"The lug nuts. You seem to be indicating you have an idea who tampered with the vehicle."

"He took my laptop and notebook."

"Who?"

Jack paused to think. He was a stranger here. For all he knew, Vic Loew and Rhett Tackett went to high school together. Maybe they were drinking buds. They went trap shooting. Or, once the story was told, maybe Tackett would agree that Jack had been out of line when he interviewed Victor Loew at the senior home. It's been a long time since journalists got the benefit of the doubt in America.

"I'm feeling like I need a lawyer," Jack said. "My brain took a jolt out there."

"I'm just trying to find out what happened," Tackett said.

Before Tackett turned up, Jack had the wit to take a selfie of his face: purple in the center, puffy all around, black eyes on their way. Borderline gruesome. The sling spoke for itself, as did the metal splint on the middle finger of his right hand.

"I don't mean any disrespect," Jack said. "Let me organize my thoughts."

"We're going to want to talk to you before you leave town." Tackett stood. He handed him a card.

Jack's roommate let out another bestial snore.

Jack went into his contacts list to find a lawyer he knew would help.

"Henry," he wheezed. "It's Jack Fiorello. I'm sorry to bother you at home, but is Suzi around?"

Henry Lee said, "She's right here, Jack." I heard him whisper, "It's Jack Fiorello. I don't know. He wants to talk to you." Then, coming back to me, he said, "You sound strange. Are you all right?"

"Not too all right," Jack told him.

Suzi took up the phone. "Jack. What's going on?"

An accident. Not an accident. Deliberate. An armed security guard. Jack said he was on a story. A threat. His laptop and notebook were taken, he added. Yes, in a hospital. Broken nose, other stuff. His shoulder; maybe a concussion, maybe not. I don't know.

"Where are you?"

"Tennessee. Somewhere near Nashville"

"Tennessee?" Suzi said. "Give me the name of the hospital."

She told him to hold tight.

With the sling and splint, Jack found it almost impossible to step into his jeans, but, motivated by a desire to escape audio torture, he succeeded, his belt hanging open like a hound's tongue. Wearing the backless gown and his mud-stained sneakers, he went to the nurses' station. He took a scolding about being out of bed; pointing with his splint hand, he said, "That guy in there is a chainsaw." Just as he was about to ask to borrow a power cord, his phone rang. It was Suzi.

She said a Nashville-based attorney named Arthur Lash Jr. would be in touch.

"So soon?" he said as he limped away from the desk.

"Henry's family is connected," she said. "It's a home game for you now."

Jack recalled that Henry graduated from Northwest Prep and Vanderbilt.

"Be straight with Arthur, Jack. There's no funk in this man."

"I appreciate it, Suzi. Tell Henry I said so, OK?"

A nurse—Black, short, stout and no glad sufferer of fools—came to chase him back to bed. Jack feared she would put him under her arm and carry him to the room. But when he made his case, she proved more sympathetic than he had anticipated. With another painkiller in his blood, he was rolled in a wheelchair to the visitors' lounge with a charger, yellow legal pad and a well-chewed Bic pen. Jack set about to recreate his notes, cheese-and-peanut butter crackers and bottled water on the nearby table.

Using his phone, Jack found a photo of Arthur Lash Jr. He had neatly combed brown hair that was graying at the temples, close-set eyes, long nose and rubbery lips. He seemed to glower with indignity as if justice itself had been offended.

In his haze, it made sense to Jack that Lash called as he was staring at his picture.

"Mr. Fiorello," he said in an accent far more pronounced than any Jack had heard since he arrived in Tennessee. "We're getting you out of there."

Lash was sending an aide. Be ready, he advised.

A half-hour later, Jack was in the wide rear seat of an ink-black Escalade, a wiry, steel-eyed Black man behind the wheel. As the Cadillac eased out of the hospital parking lot, Jack's phone buzzed again. It was Lash.

"Tell me what you consider the most pertinent information, Mr. Fiorello."

"I interviewed a man, eighty-seven years old, who was involved in the death of a woman back in 1977 in New York City. He's a song thief, this man. All he's got he stole."

"Go on." Lash was taking notes.

"His son, an armed bank guard, a real shit, came to my hotel, threatened me and demanded my notes. A while later, a front tire came off the car. I slid off the road and into a ditch. Then my laptop and notebook were stolen. And here we are."

"Fortunate to be, I would say. This man, this armed guard—"

"Vic Loew."

"Vic Loew. He was in uniform when he threatened you?"

Jack said yes.

"Carrying his company-issued firearm?"

His head was throbbing. So was the dead center of his face. On the other hand, he was feeling wonderfully compliant.

"Demanded your notes, you say."

Jack didn't respond. When he tried to bring his right hand to his forehead to press against the pain, he jabbed himself with the tip of the splint.

"You're feeling poorly?"

"I am feeling very poorly," Jack agreed.

He looked out toward a highway coated in darkness. A light drizzle had begun to fall, and the driver tapped the wipers on and off.

He said, "The police want to see me."

"You need to get yourself home, Mr. Fiorello. Your own bed, your own doctor. We'll handle this. Now, let me speak to Jebby."

Jack put his phone on the driver's shoulder.

A moment or so later, Jebby returned it.

"Where am I going?" Jack asked Lash.

"Out of town," the lawyer replied. His voice seemed to come from far away. "Anything else?"

"My laptop. My notes. An apology."

"Oh, you will get more than an apology, Mr. Fiorello. Allow me to assure you of that."

In a hotel suite outside of Knoxville, Jack was tended to through the night by Jebby, Coiled in black slacks, a black T and a black parachute jacket, Jebby stationed himself in an arm chair facing the door, his eyes shifting. Jack, door, Jack, door. Later, Jack was told Jebby was wearing a gun.

At one point, he woke Jack with a gentle nudge.

"Sorry," he said. "Pill time."

Just about everything hurt, including places that hadn't hurt before. Jebby handed him two painkillers and a glass of water.

"Tell me about you," said Jack, who blinked to concentrate.

Turned out that Jebby had played football at the University of Tennessee until he was hit so hard that he needed emergency surgery to remove a kidney. His mother was a paralegal at Lash, Hollenbeck and Rye, which sued the NCAA, the Southeastern Conference, the university and equipment manufacturers—"Everybody but me and the dog," Jebby summarized. His mother decided he should study law and Jebby saw the wisdom in her thinking. He was interning at the firm.

"You're a charmer," Jack told Jebby, "a good storyteller. You're going to do all right."

Jebby shrugged.

Jack dropped off to sleep and came back around when he heard a phone ring. Molly, he thought. But it turned out he and Jebby had the same ringtone.

"We're leaving," Jebby said.

Jack stared with pin-wheeling eyes. "Bathroom," Jack said, as he struggled to stand. "Old-man bladder."

"You might want to check on that scar on the side of your head," said Jebby, hiding a grimace.

Looking in the mirror, Jack saw he was worse off than he had been before, his face a riot of yellows and purples, bumps and bulges. Some kind of slime was oozing through his stitches. My brain is leaking, thought Jack as he dabbed at the wound with a wad of tissues.

Jebby handed him a toothbrush and toothpaste. He said, "We've got to get going."

Despite the murky clouds in his mind, Jack understood Lash assumed Vic Loew was going to come after him again.

Jebby loaded Jack and his duffel bag into the elevator. Jack wore his leather coat like a cape.

In the lobby, Jack saw night hadn't fully passed.

"This way," Jebby said, steering him.

He put Jack in the black Escalade's back seat and made a pillow out of his duffel.

"Sleep," Jebby instructed as he turned over the engine and looked into the rearview.

Jack wondered if he could remove the sling. Instead, he rolled into a fetal position with his left arm on top. "Where are we going?" he asked.

"A drive. You got time."

Jebby rolled up to the lip of the hotel parking garage, looking to see who might be ready to tail them and then pressed on. When he was convinced that they were all right, he motored steadily toward Route 40, heading east. For the next three-and-a-half hours, as night faded to a pale, watery blue, he drove carefully, watching for anyone who followed him with deliberation, dark, wary eyes in the rearview. Twice, he exited only to get right back on the interstate.

They arrived at Charlotte Douglas Airport after sun-up but with the sky muted and gray. Jebby found a spot not far from a terminal.

"Jack," he said.

Jack didn't stir.

Jebby hopped out of the Escalade, opened the back door and tugged Jack by his mud-stained sneaker.

"Let's go," he ordered.

Jack came to. His body screamed in pain.

Jebby, he thought. That man in black is Jebby.

Slowly, carefully, Jack sat upright. He moaned low and then he let out a little squeak-squeal.

Looking at Jebby, he said, "There is nothing about this that I enjoy."

A jet roared on takeoff. Charlotte Douglas was a busy airport, a hub. Jack had flown in and out of it several times. I'm in Charlotte, thought Jack.

Jebby offered to lift him onto his feet, but Jack managed by himself. Jebby told Jack to lock arms with him. We'll walk slowly, he added, carrying the duffel and Jack's coat.

Jack noted that Jebby was made of tempered steel.

Jebby looked over Jack's head to examine the lot. People hurried to catch their flights, rolling bags tailing them. No one seemed to be watching Jack.

"Ready?"

"Don't make me lie," Jack replied.

They took baby steps, but soon, they gathered a bit of momentum.

Jack felt the cold morning air on his face. The glass terminal was a very big diamond that was moving toward him and then slipping away.

"You talk in your sleep," Jebby told him as they waited for traffic to pass.

"Do I?"

"Who's Katy?" Jebby asked.

Jebby handed Jack to a gate agent. In gratitude, Jack gave Jebby a little hug, more or less just circling him with his free hand. The simple gesture made his body erupt in pain.

"The change in cabin pressure might do you in," said the gate agent, who had grimaced at the sight of Jack's battered face.

Jebby stayed behind as Jack was led toward security, his duffel on a rolling cart. At Lash's instructions, he watched until Jack disappeared.

Carrying Jack's coat, the agent steered him past rows of white rocking chairs. Passengers sat and lingered as if they had hours until boarding time. Jack couldn't make sense of it. He caught a whiff of barbecue and then gestured to a Jamba Juice stand.

"I might enjoy that," Jack told the agent. His throat was parched, his stomach queasy. He was thinking it was past time to drop another painkiller.

No juice, she said with a smile. "We're going to get you situated."

When they came to an intersection—one terminal this way, another that way, a third requiring a sharp right turn—Jack asked to pause. His aching ribs made it difficult to breathe.

People were staring at his face.

The agent waited patiently. She was small and stocky with a hairdo like Diana Ross wore with the Supremes. Ross wasn't on "Nathan Jones" and "Up the Ladder to the Roof," Jack's favorite Supremes' tracks, but Jack Ashford was. Quick, name another tambourine player.

"You are a pro," Jack said to the agent.

Soon, they arrived at the Admirals Club, a lounge dedicated to business- and first-class passengers. It occurred to a deeply dulled Jack that he was flying someplace.

The gate agent pushed open the door.

And Jack saw Henry Lee standing by the check-in desk.

His face knit with concern, Henry rushed forward. "Jack, Jack," he said softly. "You're all right now."

No, no, thought Jack. Not all right.

"Henry. What's going on?"

"I'm going to take you home," he said.

Henry accepted the coat from the agent, who then presented Jack's ticket to her colleagues. Jack thanked her as she departed.

"There's a pill in there," Jack said, pointing his splint toward the duffel. "I hope."

Henry pulled back the zipper and began to rummage.

"The Supremes had eight Top 40 hits after Ross split," Jack said as he began to crumble to the carpeted floor. "Did you know that?"

They were seated in first class, Jack next to the window. The remaining passengers who boarded stared at the bruised and sagging man as they shuffled along the aisle.

Jack had taken a painkiller and his body felt a little better. But his thoughts were tones that adhered to no scale. He asked Henry if his brain was still leaking.

The steward had taken Henry's topcoat and scarf, but Jack had his coat across his lap. For some reason, the weight felt comforting. Maybe it would keep him from floating away.

Somewhere high in the mid-Atlantic sky, Jack cleared his throat and said, "Henry. What's going on?"

Henry placed his *Forbes* magazine on his tray next to his coffee cup.

"You've been hurt bad," he said, leaning close to Jack. "Suzi and I just wanted to make sure you got home all right." He smiled sympathetically.

"But you didn't—I mean, did you have to come?"

"What are friends for?"

Friends? "Am I in trouble? None of this is making sense."

"Well, according to Arthur," Henry replied, "we're acting on the assumption that someone tried to kill you."

Jack sighed. With his thumb and index finger, he lifted his glass of orange juice and took a sip.

Henry said, "You'll tell us what's going on when you're ready."

"A girl died. A musician. Talented. Fighting the good fight. They stole her music. The police said suicide. I don't think so…there are things…strains, threads. Things."

Lash had told Henry as much.

"In 1977," Jack added.

"Long time ago," said Henry.

"I haven't figured out if that's so," Jack replied. "Time is what? I don't know…here, there. Born, die. Needed, not. Days dwindle. Do they?" He sighed as he nodded off. "I got nothing…"

Chapter Thirteen

Suzi was waiting at baggage claim at La Guardia.

"Oh dear god," she said, lifting her sunglasses.

She wore big red pearls, a chartreuse blouse with silver studs for buttons, a green skirt, green cowboy boots and a silver Apple watch. In his haze, Jack thought she looked like a Christmas tree.

Holding Jack by his elbow, Henry shrugged sheepishly. "He's having a rough time," he told his wife.

"Water," Jack said. "I'm dry as dust."

As people lingering for their luggage stared, Henry lugged Jack's muddy duffel and walked him to the fountain. Bending down made Jack's head pound.

"Whoa," Jack said as he wobbled.

"Should I get a wheelchair?"

"My humiliation would then be complete." He looked at her. "But thank you. Thanks, Suzi. Henry. Really. I didn't expect—Suzi?"

"Jack, you look really awful. Brutal," she said. "I'm glad Molly's coming home."

"Wait. That's not—"

"I tracked her down—with the help of Oxfam."

"I wanted to wait to see if I was—"

"What? Dead? We're not arguing, Jack."

Meek sunlight flooded the lower level. Flanked by Suzi and Henry, Jack started tottering toward the exit. "We're documenting it," said Suzi. "Jack, you could've been killed."

Jack agreed. "I could have been killed."

"What for? Is it worth it?"

"Yes," he replied.

The limo had been waiting, its engine purring; inside, the driver had the heat on high. Suzi sat next to Jack in the back seat. Henry went in next to the driver. Immediately, both started working. As if to conform, Jack thought to check his phone, but removing it from his pocket with his splinted hand proved too difficult.

Traffic was at a standstill on the Grand Central Parkway. On her call, Suzi was responding with brevity: "Yes." "That's fine." "Push it back."

Jack was surprised to hear Henry conducting his conversation in German.

The car inched ahead. Jack flexed his left hand. He rolled his arm around. Dislocated shoulder was back in place and the residual pain was bearable. But every breath was minor torture.

Call ended, Suzi turned to Jack on the soft leather seat. She told him Lash not only wanted the photos, but also a detailed transcription of his recollections, preferably by this afternoon.

"About your confrontation with the armed guard…" she said.

"Vic Jr. He's a bad guy, Suze. Call Blunderbuss Studios. Milton Klinger. And the receptionist. They know. They'll tell you."

"I'll let Arthur know. People understand there's a different kind of hell to pay with him. But he's not going ahead without a narrative."

Henry turned to give his wife a knowing glance.

Jack said, "There are notes on a yellow pad in…." He stopped. "Jesus, my head is spinning." Then: "What do you mean—'hell to pay'?"

"Jack, you're buying Molly a home on Lake Como." The limo driver darted to change lanes. "You're sitting at the head table."

Jack couldn't respond. It hadn't occurred to him that getting smashed in a car wreck could be a good thing.

"And leverage this as a journalist," she added. "What did you say? A woman died? Copyright issues? A song thief? And they came after you. A near-fatal vehicular assault."

"'Vehicular,' said Jack.

"Somebody fucked up, Jack. We're not having it." She made a little wiggly gesture with her finger. "Your nose is bleeding."

They spent hours in Suzi's office near the Flatiron Building. The photographer came and went; at Suzi's insistence, she took many photos of the wound on the side of Jack's head. "How does that happen if the airbag hit you so squarely that your nose was broken?" she asked. Click, click went the photographer. "Does he need another blow to ensure you're out long enough so he can steal your notes?"

Next, Suzi interrogated Jack in the presence of a stenographer. She took down everything he remembered about Vic Loew and his threats. Then he tried to eat a tuna sandwich on rye, but his jaw ached too much to chew. He finally ate the tuna with a plastic spoon and washed it down with seltzer.

As miserable as he felt, he was better than he had been.

"We'll check in on you later," Suzi said as she walked him to the elevator, hand on his back.

"No need. Just send my notes, OK? I'm turning off the phone." Again, he said, "Thank Henry for me. You guys were great. I couldn't have done it alone."

Suzi scanned Jack's face. "Looking for a place to kiss…" she said.

"Bottom lip."

Suzi ordered a car to take him home. The driver looked at Jack and shook his head when he held open the back door. As they swept toward the FDR, Jack peered at Brooklyn and saw a razor-thin tower that wasn't there last week. He nodded off to sleep and he wasn't fully awake when he stepped out of the car on Chambers on the corner of Broadway.

Jack dropped his duffel and coat. The door closed behind him with a thud.

Gingerly, timidly, he removed his arm from the sling and flexed it as if he were holding a dumbbell. Trudging across the apartment, he hoisted it as high as it could go without a stab of pain. He put the empty sling on Molly's chair. He tapped his splinted finger on the kitchen counter.

Jack sat at his desk, facing the space where his laptop would usually be.

After a while, he stood and he felt a jab of pain in his shoulder. He crooked his arm and pressed it to his chest. Better.

He sat on the sofa, facing "Fleeing Ghost" and "Tänzerin." His head bobbed.

When he woke, he was a mess. Everything hurt. He brought his hand to his face. Caked blood under his nose. Jack found the orange plastic container amid his soiled clothes. His supply was already running low.

He felt a wave of nausea and stumbled toward the bathroom. He gagged, but no more. He stood in place for several minutes, hands on the cool sink. It wasn't as if he couldn't decide what to do. He didn't even consider that he needed to decide what to do. What was happening? Jack didn't know.

"I need a shower. No," said Jack, "I need sleep."

He took two pills.

He produced his phone to check his voicemail.

Molly.

"Jack, I'm in Zurich. Are you all right? Call if you want. Jack, you…my Jack."

With his right index finger only, he wrote an email to his wife: "Are you still in Europe? No need to return. I'm under Suzi's care. My nose is the color of an eggplant, but it's OK. I'm sorry to disrupt your good work. Goodnight, Zurich."

Jack sat on the sofa, careful not to jar his shoulder. A siren in the distance. Approaching the Brooklyn Bridge? Dozy, drooping, he looked at Klee's "Tänzerin," the happy dancer.

"Katy? Katy, were you happy when you thought you had finally gotten your break? Did you dance with joy at a bar in Nashville?"

Jack struggled to sit up.

"Ah, Katy," he moaned. "Nobody had the right."

Jack slept fitfully. The pinch and punch he felt on his wounded shoulder woke him repeatedly. His ribs were barbed wire. Twice during the dark night, he revisited the kitchen for painkillers. They had an appeal that worried him, giving him a golden glow, a woozy contentment. His mind became amendable. Edgard Varèse made sense. So did a fleet of hot-air balloons over the Arizona mesas.

He decided to get out of bed, though his ribs screamed in protest. He whistled through his nose when he breathed. No blood in his pee, as he feared. Brushing his teeth wasn't a torture because, at some point during the night, he had decided to remove the splint, though he couldn't remember when. His shower was a modest joy, as was the slice of cold pepperoni pizza he found in the fridge.

He sent a text to Suzi: "All's well. Thanks again for yesterday. Too kind."

He wondered if he was fit enough to get himself to the Apple Store in Soho to buy a new laptop. He could pull a knit cap over the wound on the side of his head. His face—

Jack heard the hallway door open. He waited, looking like a teen's messy bedroom in his saggy socks, jeans and an old boolah-boolah button-down sweater. He heard the rattle of a roller luggage.

Molly stepped into the apartment.

"Hey!" said Jack with genuine glee.

When she saw her husband, Molly let out a gasp. And then she started to cry.

"No, no, no," Jack said, skating to her. "It's not as bad as it—Molly, no." He took her hands and raised them to his face. "Much better already," he told her.

Molly leaned her chin against his shoulder. He rubbed her back.

"Suzi said someone tried to hurt you."

"Indeed. Did it, too."

She dabbed her nose with a paper towel. "In Tennessee. Why?"

Jack concealed a grimace as he rolled Molly's luggage toward the bedroom.

"Jack?"

"I was in Nashville, chasing down an idea for an article," he said. "It started to spiral. Got out of hand too fast."

Molly was puzzled. "Not for *The Observer*..."

Jack said no. "Katy Shayne. Remember?" He felt a ripple of pain through his midsection and let out a little gasp. As he gripped the back of his stool, he said, "They killed her, Molly. Somebody did."

He explained. He interviewed a man, quite elderly, who revealed that he had concealed information that might be related to Katy's death. His son, a rent-a-cop, a douchebag, came after him to get his notebook and laptop. Twice. Once he threatened, next he took action.

"Henry Lee knows people in Tennessee. There's a lawyer down there looking into it. Arthur Lash. I spoke to the police. It's a thing that happened."

"You're shaking. You're pale."

"My ribs. They're the worst of it, I guess."

"Your hair. You look halfway—"

"Stitches. They don't hurt." He forced a smile as he held up his hand. "I dislocated a finger. They fixed it."

She hesitated. "No need for that, Jack."

"What?"

"No need to sell me. You were hurt bad. You could've been killed."

"Wasn't, though."

"Don't be flip."

"I'm just trying—"

"This is bullshit, Jack," she said with surprising force. "You know that, don't you?"

"Whoa," said Jack. "What— You're tired."

"Thirty-something years with *The Observer* and not so much as a hangnail. Now this?" She pointed toward his constellation of bruises, gashes and scars. "We're not shrugging it off. Oh no, Jack. No, we are not."

She had her fists on her hips.

"I don't know why, in God's name, you think you have to do this," she said. "To impress *the Observer*? Your old boss?"

"Molly..."

Red-faced, she marched toward him. "Your mother, Jack? A teacher who wasn't kind?"

"Hey. Enough, all right?"

"Not enough, Jack. You almost got yourself killed and for what? Tell me,

Jack. For what?"

Nausea rising, he walked away. Molly grabbed him by the bicep. "God damn it, you don't have to do this, Jack. You don't."

He turned. "Oh, yes, I do. I do. It's a story. A good one. Something is at stake. Really. I mean, look at me. Somebody thought the story needed to be killed bad enough to do this."

"That's my point, Jack. Who's going to write your In Memoriam if you get killed? No one. Who is this important to? Besides you, who?"

"Molly, I hear you, OK?"

"Not OK—"

"I ask you as calmly as I can: Please stop."

"Not until you tell me why, Jack. Why is this so important to you?"

He bowed his head and stared at the hardwood floor.

"No, Jack. I want to hear it. Tell me why—"

"Because I'm afraid," he said, looking at her. "I'm sixty-five years old and I have nothing to do with the rest of my life. Because unless I'm working, I'm nothing, Molly. I'm that kid in his room in Queens who's scared shitless that he's buried under his mother's insanity and his father's defeat and he'll never get out. And I'm alone, Molly. Just like I was in my neighborhood, in my school, anywhere. Alone. Except I've got this gift: to listen, to take it in, to write, to share. You understand?

"You're alone, Jack? Is that what you're saying?"

"Damn it. You know what I mean. If I don't reclaim my life, Molly, I'm going to dry up and blow away. Without my work, I am nothing."

She leaned back, a quizzical expression locked on her face. "Jack, how can you say that to me? You're my husband, you're my—"

"Believe me, Molly, you wouldn't have given that kid in Queens a second thought." He leaned against the pillar. "But I figured it out. I could be somebody, *anybody*, else. I invented me, Molly. Then I went after it and I got it and I'm at the best newspaper in the country, me, and oh look, here's Molly—Oliwia Kraska from Wroclaw, Poland—with a loving mother who brought her to freedom, an opportunity to study, M.A. and driven and a presence and what have I done to earn her? What does she see in me? I swore

I would never disappoint this woman, this miraculous woman whose eyes seem to light up when I enter a room. Me. Jack Fiorello. I'm lovable?"

"Jack—"

"And meanwhile, not a week went by when some hot-shot from Columbia J School or Madison or USC or some mid-sized newspaper or a blog didn't try to take my job. They wanted to erase me. But they had no idea how dug in I was. You really think *The New National Observer* needed a rock critic? I made it happen, Molly, by force of will, and I did it right. Never made a deal, never fucked over a source, never fudged a single quote in my entire career. My reward? Teeter-totter the fuck out, old man.

"And so, no. No. No. I'm not done. I'm not done. All right? You ask: Why is this story so important to me? Aside from standing up for an earnest, hard-working girl from New Jersey with real talent who got eaten up and spit out by the machine that didn't give a good God damn about her dreams, her mission, her songs?

"It's important to me because without an objective, without the honor of connecting reader and artist, the reader and the song, I am *nothing*."

He pointed at her. "And you, who I love more than I thought possible, deserve better than some vanishing sack of skin and bones. And after a lifetime of work, I deserve better too. The thing I went after and got? I'm not letting go. Fuck that. I am not letting go."

Stunned, Molly stared without a word. Then she burst into tears.

Jack said, "Yeah. Right. There it is. OK?'

He retreated to his office, hoping the nausea would pass, realizing that his head was about to explode and his ribs were going to burst through his skin.

When he came out, whenever it was, Molly was staring down at the traffic on Broadway.

The old axiom "never go to bed angry" did not apply to the Fiorello marriage, so it wasn't until the morning that Jack, who slept on the sofa, said, "Forgive me?"

"We need to clarify a few things," she replied from the kitchen without looking at him. She had showered but was still in her robe.

He wore gray sweats and a shabby T that read "Stupid Dream." Sometime during the night, he lost a sock. There was oozy blood on his pillow.

"Whatever bothers you the most is likely something that came out wrong," he said. "Our marriage means the world to me. You mean the world to me."

"I can deal with Old Jack," she said, waiting for the kettle to whistle. "I'm not ready yet for Dead Jack."

Old Jack inched gingerly toward the counter. On his back, he hadn't felt half bad. Moving revived the pain in full force.

"I've got to work, babe," he said, trying to stand tall.

"So I've been told." She left the kitchen. "You're in pain."

Molly volunteered to help him undress and followed him as he dragged himself into the bathroom. When she lifted his T, she gasped. His torso was a parade of ghastly colors.

"Good God in heaven," she said. "Are you sure you're all right?"

"Not sure. But they said I'd heal so…"

When she heard the shower water turn off, she joined him in the steamy bathroom to help him dry. Two cups of steaming tea waited on the counter.

"I actually feel better," he said. "Maybe. Somewhat."

She dabbed his back. "You'll be Jack again."

"And that's good?"

She ignored the comment, pointed to his privates and handed him the towel.

Jack liked charts. He kept a pad of graph paper in his desk and would say proudly that he had never, not once, used Microsoft Excel. Now, he was hunched over his latest: Songs Victor Loew claimed to have composed or co-composed; who recorded them; when. Many had been cut by Grady Tell. But nine were recorded in 1973 by Babs White, a country singer out of Alabama whose lone album appeared on no streaming services. She had no Wiki page, no website. And no obituary yet for Babs White, but a profile in *the Decatur Daily* celebrated Barbara Hochman Schneider, Morgan County Realtor of the Year for 2013. It wasn't Ms. Hochman Schneider's first brush with excellence, said the *Daily*. She had done Huntsville proud as the teen sensation Babs White—formerly Lil' Babs White—who, at age 18 gave up a very promising career in music to attend the University of North Alabama.

He located the phone number for Schneider-Hamilton Realty.

"Schneider-Hamilton."

"Hi, I'm looking for Ms. Hochman Schneider."

"Speaking."

"Ms. Schneider, my name is Jack Fiorello. I'm a journalist you may know from *The New National Observer…*"

After a perfunctory hello, Molly went into the kitchen to poach salmon and steam green beans. From his office, Jack asked about her day, but stayed away. She was still miffed, he knew, probably rightly so. They listened to NPR as they ate.

"Did you talk to Suzi?" she asked finally.

He shook his head. "You?"

She had not, no.

"I worked the phone, though," he said as he gathered the dishes. "Day flew by."

She brought her wine glass to the sofa. She was on her second glass of Sauvignon Blanc when Jack returned to his stool to tell her about Babs White.

"So I ask her: 'What can you tell me about Victor Loew?' She says: 'That he's a son of a bitch.'

"Turns out thirteen-year-old Babs and her father had gone to Nashville in 1971 with a bunch of tunes they had written. They bounced around, generated little interest and then ran into Loew and Morningside Publishing. He signed them, brought Babs into the studio and cut her debut album. When he gave them a copy, they saw he had listed the songs as composed by the Whites and Loew. She said he didn't add so much as a note or word to the tunes."

The wine had taken a bit of the chill out of the air. Molly had turned to face him. Jack was unaware that she was often more entertained by his adventures in reporting than by his actual articles.

"So, she's no Teresa Brewer. The album tanks. By then, Babs and her father have had just about enough of Nashville. They return home and resume gigging around the county. Couple of years pass, Babs finishes high school, goes off to college and that's that.

"Except in 1991, Swanson Seagull has a hit with a ballad 'Our Last Morning Coffee.'" Jack stood and paced gingerly. "'Coffee' makes the Billboard country charts. Swanson Seagull tours with Alabama, with George Strait, gets some TV time—a nice career boost. Meanwhile, Babs White, now Barbara Hochman Schneider, hears it and knows immediately it's "Tuscaloosa Sunrise," a song she wrote with her father at the kitchen table when she was a kid. She gets a copy of Billboard and sees two composers are listed. And she isn't one of them."

"What did she do about it?"

"Wait. There's a twist."

"Just one? I'm teasing." She was sitting cross-legged now. "Go on."

"One composer was Victor Loew, of course. The other: Alan A. Carpenter. Now of the Eldridge Guitar Shop on the Lower East Side. Briefly, Katy Shayne's guitarist. And after that, a member of Swanson Seagull's backing band."

"He's involved."

Jack nodded. "He's the man who persuaded Katy to go to Nashville. He probably told Loew Swanson Seagull he needed material. Loew dug up Babs' song. He and Carpenter rewrote the lyrics."

"Did she sue?"

"Babs? No. She said she didn't want to step back into that world. Everything worked out fine for her—better than if she made it in music: kids, career, community. Though when I told her, Victor Loew was still alive...well, she didn't say 'Bless his heart.'"

He winched. Ribs again and now the side of his head hurt, too.

"Maybe call it a day, Jack?"

"I'm pumped. Adrenaline. Before I crash, I want to try to track down the other songs attributed to Loew. Maybe see if the recording artists knew he was shady."

She tapped the soft cushion. "Fine. At least let me change that bandage on your head."

"No, it's—"

"It's disgusting, Jack. Let me take care of it."

He slumped to the sofa. Cradling hydrogen peroxide, gauze pads, tape, scissors and a face cloth, Molly returned to the living room to find Jack asleep, chin to chest.

Chapter Fourteen

J ack entered the venue, unfurled his scarf and unzipped his old leather coat as he settled in a back corner near the ATM. He dug into his pocket for a pen, opened his notebook and, tucked away from the crowd, set to go to work.

The house lights dimmed. The crowd cheered as the band took the stage, walking through darkness to their instruments. She was out front, her trademark black Fender Jaguar already in place. On his toes, Jack saw, on a stand, by the kick drum, her Guild D-40.

With a stacked heel, she set the tempo. Then, as if cracking a whip, her guitarist ripped into the riff that opened "You Can't Go Back." The drums kicked in, the stage lights exploded, and a spotlight found her: Katy Shayne. Black leather jacket, an electric blue T torn at the collar, heart-shaped pendant dangling, skintight jeans, scuffed boots.

She leaned into the mike. "Wake up and turn on the light," she sang, her voice a tad raspy and just right. "Put an end to the dead and the night."

Her shoulder-length black hair framed her angular face. Those cheekbones. That glare. Right hand pumping her pick across the six strings.

"I won't argue and I don't want to fight / Put an end to the dead and the night."

Her backing band members were grizzled veterans—gray hair under truckers' caps, torn denim, boots. The bass player wore silver skull rings and a Rolling Stones tongue T. As thin as a reed, the lead guitarist's sleeveless shirt revealed a tiger tattoo on his bicep. The quartet dug in with brutal efficiency as Katy ripped into the bridge:

"You can't go back, you cannot run away / You can't renege on the statement you gave."

Good God, Katy Shayne and the Black Canyon City Band had it tonight. Jack knew it. And Katy knew it. "You Can't Go Back" blazed, soaring relentlessly to its peak. As it roared to its end, the crowd howled and stomped. Stepping back, Katy could not conceal her delight. A thin smile, a twinkle in her eyes, an appreciative nod, a cute little wave.

A roadie appeared to take the Jaguar. Katy slipped on the Guild D-40.

"This is a tune I wrote when I was only a child," she said. "Yep, it's mine. We call it 'That Didn't Last Too Long.'"

The drummer, who had taken up brushes, counted down in double time.

Katy strummed an E chord, and the band kicked in. More bite than the Eagles gave "Peaceful Easy Feeling," for sure. Country pop with an edge.

"Just the other night, I was thinking of you / Isn't it amazing what a little thought can do?"

So good. Just right.

You took it back, Katy. You told them all to go straight to hell.

Good for you, Katy Shayne. You did it.

Katy, you did it.

Jack was asleep in an ocean of comforters and, given his battered body, Molly didn't know how to wake him. Finally, she snapped her fingers above his face.

"Get up slowly, Jack. Easy…"

He waited, taking several long breaths. His ribs jabbed as he tossed off the unruly blankets.

Limping toward the bathroom, he waved hello to Molly who by now was at the kitchen stove. In a navy skirt and sky-blue blouse, she was stirring oatmeal. She offered to make Jack a bowl, holding high a plump strawberry.

He thought to say: "Lucinda Williams and Buick 6. Katy and her band were as great as that. Really. Rattled the walls and then was as soothing as silk. She did it."

Instead, he asked: "Up long?" He'd noticed it wasn't quite daylight in New

York.

"Not too," she said. "I had a conference call with Oxfam's Oxford office."

Through the fog, Jack calculated the time difference. She might have been up since four o'clock.

In the mirror above the sink, he saw blood had caked around his nostrils.

"How are your ribs?" she asked.

"They hate me." When he coughed, a sword went through one side and came out the other.

"Suzi keeps calling."

After he washed up, vigorously here, gingerly there, and brushed his teeth and remaining hair, Jack found Molly working in his office, her papers in brightly colored folios branded with the Geo Strategic Communications logo.

"I'll put Suzi on speaker," he said, phone in hand. Seconds later: "Good morning. Molly is here with me."

Suzi said hi in a manner that suggested there would be no friendly this and that, at least not right away.

"Jack, an update: The police questioned Vic Loew."

"The armed guard," Jack whispered to his wife.

"He denies threatening you. Denies tampering with your car. Denies he stole your notebook and laptop. A witness places him at the bank when the accident occurred."

"Not an accident," Jack said. "Who's this witness? The bank had three tellers. Did they all say they saw him?"

He put the phone on the desk. When Molly offered him his chair, he waved her off.

"He could have hired someone to precipitate the event," Suzi said.

"Did they talk to the woman from Housekeeping?" Jack asked. "Any footage from the security cameras at the hotel?"

Suzi said, "Arthur isn't likely to miss anything. It's our lawyer in Nashville, Molly, via Henry's family. Your husband is in good hands. Now, Jack, listen… How do you feel?"

"Improved." He looked down at Molly and shrugged.

"Did you say awful? You can't concentrate? Vision blurry. Headaches. Constant pain. Jack, go to an emergency room. You may have a concussion after all."

"Suzi…"

"Arthur and I hope you will be able to resume your work at some point. But who knows when?"

"I'll keep an eye on him," Molly said amicably.

"A leash too. Jack, stay home. Don't get your photo taken in a club. Sleep. Tend to yourself."

They signed off. Jack put the phone in the pocket of his pajama bottoms, which sagged under the added weight.

"Subtext?" Molly asked him.

"Apparently, you're getting a home in Lake Como, courtesy of the Wilson Bank & Trust. Or someplace. Or you can give it all away to a registered charity."

A doctor was a good idea, she said. "Let's nudge Henry and see if Pfizer can help Jack get an appointment right away."

What Jack really wanted was to get back to working the story. He was going to track down Loew's history of thievery. He had a handful of surviving musicians to call, including one who knew how a Babs White tune wound up credited to Loew and Carpenter: Swanson had died a few years back, but Seagull—Herman Segal, originally from Caribou, Maine—was still alive and teaching high school chemistry. Jack had been thinking about Katy and Babs White. He knew Katy wouldn't have walked away after Loew did her wrong, as Babs and her father did. By now, Jack was sure Katy would've gone after the song thief who earned big on the efforts of others.

As Molly gathered her papers, they heard his phone buzz.

"Well, Suzi's nothing if not persistent." Then, looking at the caller ID, he said, "It's *The Observer*. Reinhard."

"Jack, we need to see you," Reinhard said directly.

"Sure. What's up?"

"Can you come in this morning?"

Jack looked at the clock in the cable box.

"Eleven o'clock," said Reinhard before Jack could answer. He told him to report to the office of deputy editorial page director, Noble Leggett.

"OK…" said Jack. He knew Leggett, but not well. An Australian, she had come over from *the Times of London* after the acquisition. She had a photo of Bono and the Edge on her credenza but turned Jack down when he tried to offload a U2 boxed set he'd received. Among her assignments was intercepting major problems before they reached Gideon Bibbage, the editor of the editorial page—her boss as well as Reinhard's.

Jack said, "What's the issue?"

"We'll see you at eleven."

By now, Molly was back in the kitchen. "Everything all right?"

"I think I'm in trouble."

"For what?"

Jack shrugged. "No idea."

"Bring Suzi."

Topcoat and black blazer over a white shirt and black jeans, Jack headed out. A painkiller had dulled the hot poker xylophoning his ribs, but it had been difficult to walk in rhythm. Dropping the key as he tried to lock the front door, he let out a yelp as he bent to retrieve it.

Once settled in the car service's backseat, Jack prepared his defense for a crime that had yet to be revealed, searching his woozy brain for acts of guilt. Then he reminded himself that he was the aggrieved party: He hadn't asked to leave. He didn't kick himself out. In a just world where decisions were made on the basis of capability and commitment rather than an arbitrary figure—if 70 is the new 50, why isn't 65 the new 45?—he'd be working a story for his column. He was intrigued by the new James Blake due in mid-January and, prior to his ouster, had scheduled a phoner for next week. He was finally going to do a feature on a power trio from Switzerland that made great music, but hadn't broken through in the U.S. Based on a rough cut he'd been given, he was already in love with the forthcoming Weyes Blood album and put *The Observer* first in the queue for interviews. None of it was going to happen through no fault of his own and now he was being summoned to face a tribunal?

Jack was growing increasingly defiant. "Noble, are you cooking up some allegations so you can void the contract?" "Was I supposed to whimper away just because management wanted me to?" "Look at me and tell me I lost my mojo, Noble. Show me any evidence that indicates I could no longer do the job."

Battling westbound traffic and tsunamis of jaywalkers, the long black car finally arrived at *The Observer*'s brown-brick headquarters, whose costly refurbishing eliminated its history as a warehouse of a horse-drawn buggy manufacturer. Jack groped with his foot for the curb. Only twenty degrees, the brisk air felt good on his battered face, but he was in no mood for cheer. Limping toward the entrance, he was snapped to by Suzi, who trotted toward him. She reached to shake his hand.

"Easy. Finger."

They managed a clumsy sideways five.

Suzi was in her long red down coat and wore her pink knit cap with pointy cat's ears. "Do you feel anywhere near as bad as you look?" she asked.

In the car, Jack crooked his arm and held it in place with his free hand. "Depends on how bad I look."

"More yellow than purple," she said, scrutinizing. "An improvement. Are you up for this?"

"I'm miffed. Insulted. 'Get your ancient ass over here, Jack.' Why? I thought we had a deal."

"We do."

"Yet we're perp walking."

"Not really. But I understand. You're hurt. But let's listen. Big conglomerate. Little rock critic. Let's see what they have to say."

He hesitated. "You're a provocation."

She smiled, lifted her sunglasses, and winked. "I am, aren't I?"

She went first through the revolving door. Seconds later, as he attempted to bring her to the elevator, he found that his security badge had been deactivated.

The deputy editorial page director's office was deemed too small for the meeting. They were instructed to proceed to a conference room that had a view of the traffic on Varick. In deference to his injury, Suzi helped Jack take off his coat. Then she removed hers. She wore a violet windowpane sweater dress and sparkly gray hose. In the elevator, she had replaced her flats with black high heels. Slipping a leather folio out of her briefcase, she said, "Let's go to work."

They walked past the edit-page administrative staff, all fully occupied. Jack felt a sudden need for acknowledgment. He was hoping someone would at least nod.

"You're seeing this?" Jack whispered. "Am I invisible?"

"Sssh. Put on your game face."

Lee Reinhard was already in the room, seated close to the head of the table in his customary frumpy suit and Harvard tie. He recoiled at the sight of Jack's bruises and the gauze pad on the side of his badly shaved head. Then he greeted Suzi with austere professionalism.

He asked what had happened.

"Someone tried to kill me," Jack told him as he and Suzi sat at the other end of the six-seat table. "I'm not kidding."

Before Reinhard could ask another question, Noble Leggett arrived. Tall and imperial, Leggett had won two Walkley Awards, Australia's Pulitzer Prize, while managing editor at a small-town newspaper in Queensland. *The Observer*'s Australian ownership imported her to run a real-estate section that was a spigot of cash. People in the organization who focused on her flinty gaze and flamboyant scarves missed how diamond-sharp she could be and just how much she had achieved.

"Jack," she said with a snap.

"Good to see you again, Noble."

He introduced Suzi. "She's an attorney. An advisor."

They shook hands like competitors.

Leggett put down her folio as she settled at the head of the table. Jack expected her to begin the meeting immediately, but she waited, reviewing her notes and spinning her pen as if a drummer twirling a stick.

The waiting continued until Medgar Wells arrived. Jack was surprised to see him. Big, brassy and Black, he usually stayed on his side of the News-Editorial divide as a deputy managing editor. He and Jack had a nodding acquaintance, but Jack couldn't recall if they had ever spoken beyond a greeting in the cafeteria or elevator.

Wells, who was in rolled-up shirt sleeves, called Leggett and Reinhard by their first names. He grimaced at Jack's face and introduced himself to Suzi. Then he plopped into a chair, his back to the window onto New Jersey. "We ready?" he said, rapping a knuckle on the table. He slid his chair to close the conference room door.

"Jack," Noble Leggett said, "what are you working on."

Jack looked at his editor, who avoided his gaze.

"IMs," he replied.

"IMs," she repeated.

"Sixty-seven. Lee can confirm."

She said, "Is that a reason to tell the Davidson County Sheriff's Office that you're on assignment for *The Observer*?"

"What's that?" Jack asked, cupping an ear.

"Did you tell—"

"No, I heard you. I'm just surprised you'd believe it."

"Did you not interrogate an eighty-seven-year old man"—she looked at her notes—"a Victor Loew, telling him you were working on a piece for us?"

"I did not."

"We're told otherwise," said Leggett.

Jack could feel his indignation begin to bubble. "If you're of a mind to take the word of strangers, I can't help you."

Wells interrupted. "Jack, just tell us what you're working on."

"No, Medgar. I don't think I will."

Leggett turned to Reinhard. "Lee, tell Medgar what you know about this."

"He doesn't know anything about this," Jack interrupted. "There's no 'this.'"

Reinhard shifted nervously. "As I wrote in the email I sent Gideon, I received a call from a sheriff—"

"Rhett Tackett," Jack said. "He interviewed me in the hospital after…" Jack ran a circle near his bruised face.

Reinhard continued, "He said that Jack had interviewed Victor Loew for a story for us."

"I didn't say that. If there's a story, I'm not doing it for *The Observer*."

Leggett asked, "Did you identify yourself as a reporter for *The Observer*?"

"I'm not a reporter. I've never made that claim."

"But you told—"

"I'm sorry," Jack said firmly, "but you've been misinformed."

"You've been in contact with the New York City Police Department."

"Same deal, Noble. I never said I was working for *The Observer*. They knew my name: The cop I spoke to digs rock. Well, her father, actually."

Wells said, "To be clear, Noble, NYPD never said Jack here claimed to be working for us. Our guy at One Police Plaza wanted to know what he was up to. So I called your guy." Wells pointed to Reinhard. "On the News side, we're into conflict avoidance," he added, with a wry grin.

Leggett wasn't placated. "You threatened an eighty-seven-year-old—

"I didn't threaten—"

"You implied that you were working for *The Observer*."

Jack said, "I told his son to look me up if he needed to see if I was a journalist."

"You misrepresented—"

"Whoa, hold it. What's going on?" Jack looked at Reinhard. "Lee? I've been here thirty-seven god-damned years, and all of a sudden, I'm a liar? I'm misrepresenting myself? For what? To what end?"

"You tell us, Jack," Leggett said.

"I'm onto something and I'm working it. That's the sum of it," he replied as his anger flared. "And let's be clear, Noble: I don't owe you a damned thing."

Reinhard spoke up. "Actually, Jack, if you're working on an Arts piece, it belongs to us."

Suzi responded. "That's not so. Nowhere in the agreement is it stipulated that Mr. Fiorello is responsible to *The Observer* for anything beyond the IMs."

"If he's leveraging his relationship with the paper to secure his interviews," said Leggett, "the implication is that he's reporting for us."

"Jack," Wells said, "you're going to make me retrofit this, aren't you?"

"Make your calls, Medgar. Even down in Music City, they might say, 'Jack G. is a stand-up guy.'"

"OK, but between the cop in Davidson, the old man, and his son—"

"My gift to you, Medgar, is this: They're all full of shit. And at least two of them have a good reason to be."

He said, "You're pissed at Lee. I get that. Noble too. But what's the issue? I mean, if there's a story…"

Thought Jack: The issue? The *Observer* told me I was worthless. And had me thinking I was. But there's a young woman and her song, and maybe she saved me, and there's this light coming down from some overhead crack in the day.

And I'm alive. And as long as I'm alive…

"No issue. Lee called, I came. If you had told me Noble was going to do me like this, I would've stayed home."

He intended to bolt out of his seat, but his body wouldn't cooperate. He sort of unfolded upward, his palms on the table.

Suzi reached for his elbow. "Jack," she whispered, "your nose…"

"You know," Jack said to Leggett as he shuffled behind Wells, "my lawyer in Nashville, when he heard a guy came after me with a gun, and then a guy, maybe the same guy, ran me off the road to kill me, he didn't try to pin it on me. And he's payroll. You guys, I know most of my adult life and you do me like I stole your lunch money. Jesus."

"Jack," said Reinhard, "we're reacting to what we were told. I'm sorry if we didn't—"

"Forget it. I used to work here and now I don't. That's fine. I'm gone. Everybody's happy."

Jack headed directly to the elevators, marching as best he could. Suzi trotted to follow.

Once inside, Jack hunched over in pain.

"Jack…?"

"Fuck me," he moaned. "My ribs."

Back in their coats, Suzi's lacy handkerchief pressed against his nose, they landed in the lobby and began their slow march toward Security.

Jack was angry and he was sad. He understood this was likely the last time he would be in the building. No more drop-ins by Bootsy Collins or impromptu concerts by Bonnie Raitt. Lemmy thought Jack was going to show him a clanking printing plant and was disappointed to see yards and yards of people at computers.

Jack groaned. He dabbed at blood.

Suzi was fishing for her pink stocking cap.

They heard a voice. "Jack!"

Turning slowly, they saw Reinhard trotting across the lobby.

"We found this in a drawer."

He handed Jack a framed photo of Molly, taken on the Champs Élysées. Molly glowed with joy: She and Jack had saved enough to fly to Paris. They were kids. Everything was before them and they were invincible.

Suzi put her hand on Jack's back.

Reinhard said, "I want to apologize. I didn't know—"

Jack waved dismissively. "No worries. Maybe I put you in a bad spot."

"You'll still do the IMs…?"

"Sure. Me and the ghosts."

"You have to know I wish there could've been another way."

Jack rapped a knuckle on the Security desk. "Don't ever get old, Lee," he said. "Next thing you know, you're lying in a ditch somewhere in Tennessee."

Jack and Suzi stepped into anonymity on Varick. A policeman on horseback was slowly making his way toward a pair of limousines double-parked in front of the building. A line had formed at the gyro truck on North Moore. Jack could smell the curry and frying onions.

"Locanda Verde for lunch?" Suzi said. "I'll splurge."

"And you'll bill me."

"Well, there's that…"

Jack pointed east. "Maybe I should get home. Get my notes in order." The painkiller had just about worn off.

"It was Leggett, you know," she said. "Someone on the business side told her to find a way to cancel the agreement. Clumsy, and Wells saw right through it."

"It's a good story, Suzi."

"You want to talk about it?"

"I do not. Talking about writing is like talking about sex. It's no substitute for the doing."

"Profound, Jack." She located her sunglasses in her purse. "I'll call Arthur for an update."

"Tell him you know Tackett lied to *The Observer*. If the Sheriff's Office wants its duplicity to stay out of print, the quid is no wall around the Loews. You understand me?"

"You want to talk to the Loews again."

"Maybe. The old man should get a chance to respond."

They jaywalked across Varick. Jack waited until a taxi pulled up, said goodbye to Suzi and then held up his hand to flag another cab.

Chapter Fifteen

After downing a painkiller, Jack plopped onto the sofa. Still in his topcoat and blazer, he fell into a sort of fugue state, awake, not awake. He found it both pleasant and annoying: He wanted to be angry again but couldn't find the energy to get there.

He had no idea how long he had been in stasis when the buzzer beckoned. "China World," said the delivery man into the security camera.

Jack had no memory of calling for lunch. Apparently, he ordered four quarts of egg drop soup.

The soup cleared his head. It placated his sour stomach. He spooned down a quart while staring at the photo of Molly in Paris.

Soon, he hobbled back to the sofa to retrieve his phone. He tapped out a number down in Tennessee.

"Blunderbuss."

Jack wondered if it was the same efficient woman in orange he'd met before someone tried to kill him.

"Hi, it's Jack Fiorello. I came by the other day to talk to Milton…"

"Yes, Jack. Hold on, he's right here."

Jack heard the phone switch hands.

"This is Milt."

"Milt, Jack from New York again. Listen, I met Vic Loew."

"Lucky you," he said dryly.

"Yeah, you were dead on. Guy's a poke in the eye."

"Well, he's more than that, but go ahead."

"Do you know what he was doing before he came to work for you?"

Klinger said, "You're going to quote me?"

"Whatever I plan to run, I'll clear your quotes with you first. You say no and it's out."

"Fine," he replied. "Vic knocked around the business. Mostly for his father. He thinks he's a musician, but he's better as a tech."

"Did he ever go on the road with anybody? Maybe running sound or as a roadie?"

"Oh, for sure. He did all those things as a kid."

"With who?" Jack asked. "Do you remember?"

"Grady Tell comes to mind," Klinger said.

"Grady Tell. 'Sunday Nights and Monday Mornings.'"

"Yep. His father set him up there."

Jack's fresh red Moleskine notebook was all the way over in his office. He was scribbling on a little pad from Molly's firm.

"Do you know when that was?"

"Not for certain, no. Probably around the time 'Sunday Nights' broke out. I don't see how Grady Tell had the capital to tour national before that."

"You said he fancied himself a musician," Jack said. "What's his instrument?"

"Harmonica. He's no Mickey Raphael, though. He basically blows into the holes and hopes for the best."

"One more, Milt. When Victor Loew was producing, did he have a preferred studio?"

Klinger hummed as he thought. "Might've been Famous over in Berry Hill. But that's been gone for a good long while."

"I'm guessing I'm not going to find the records of a session back in the mid-'70s, am I?"

"Depends. Who are we talking about?"

"Katy Shayne," Jack said.

"Never heard of her."

"That's the issue. But if we're keeping secrets, Milt, she wrote a song Victor Loew ripped off."

"Wasn't 'Sunday Nights and Monday Mornings,' was it? I always thought Kristofferson wrote it and tossed it."

"It's the B side. 'Our Love Will Never Be Gone.' Check it out. It's a catchy tune."

"Well, if you're saying Victor Loew is a song thief, you're not the first."

"I'm working on that," Jack said. "Ever hear of Lil Babs White? She wrote a thing that Loew stole and turned into a hit for Swanson Seagull. There's more, no doubt."

"That's no comfort to your friend, though."

"The police think Katy killed herself right around that time."

"Damn," Klinger said. "Hold on. 'Police think'…?"

"While I have you," Jack said, moving on, "do you know who manages Grady Tell's estate?"

"'Grady Tell's estate'?"

"He must make some kind of royalties now and then."

"Grady Tell. I don't know a thing about him. Wait. Hold on."

Klinger had put his hand over the phone. Jack heard nothing but muffled conversation.

"Jack, my daughter-in-law says Grady's daughter is trying to open a—what is it?"

Jack heard the receptionist say, "CBD. Marijuana."

"—CBD Marijuana shop on Broadway Street. I'm guessing it's legal now?"

She'd need to be licensed, Jack thought.

"Bernadette. Bernadette Tell."

"This is good, Milt. Listen, you guys are golden. Keep my number, all right?"

"I've got to start reading *The Observer*, don't I?" Klinger laughed.

No sense getting into that, Jack thought as he rang off.

It was early evening now, the moon hovering over the Brooklyn Bridge. Molly had arrived with takeout borscht from Taam Tov.

"Oh, good. More soup."

They hugged. Her coat was cold, her cheeks more so. He cupped her face in his hands.

"Tough day at *The Observer*?"

"In the end, no. But it was dicey for a while."

She put down her cargo. "Suzi said you were great. Very direct."

"It had to be said," he replied. "Maybe it was a misunderstanding on Reinhard's part."

"Magnanimous Jack. That's new..."

He took Molly's laptop into his office and returned to the Village Voice archives.

Jack knew the date Katy died, so he began his search with the edition that ran the week before, looking for the quirky hand-drawn lineups the Lone Star ran in the '70s. If Vic Loew came to New York with Grady Tell in '77 for a gig at the end of May, it was likely he was here on the date she was killed.

And there it was, the lineup for the last week in May: Danny Gatton on May 27, Connie Smith, May 28, Ray Wylie Hubbard, May 29, Grady Tell, May 30.

Katy died on May 31, but the date of death begins at midnight, meaning Tell, his band and crew could've still been in New York. Even if Tell's tour bus and U-Haul-style trailers had left 13th Street within an hour or two of the show's end, Loew could have remained behind.

Jack lifted from his chair and peeked toward the kitchen. Containers of beet-red soup and a fresh loaf of rye were on the counter. Molly was changing in the bedroom or cleaning up in the bath.

"Katy," Jack whispered. "Tell me if I've got it right.

"You're furious. You see Vic Loew and confront him. Or you confront Grady Tell and Loew intervenes. Inside the Lone Star in Tell's dressing room. Out on 13th Street near the tour bus. On the bus.

"By then, you know you're not the only songwriter Loew's father ripped off.

"You went at him. Your career in jeopardy, the life you chose to lead since childhood at risk. You do not back down.

"Livid, you promise to kick Victor Loew's ass. In court.

"You'd lived with a lawyer, Katy. You knew going to court would crush the old man's reputation—rightfully so.

"Vic Loew understood. His father's reputation gone. Royalties gone. Funds that fed a family, built them a home and, four decades later, would afford an old man a place at a luxury senior center, suddenly gone. Soon, everything is gone.

"But did you know Loew had a taste for violence?"

"Jack, are you ready for dinner?" Molly shouted.

If he could track down members of Tell's band and crew, they might remember a confrontation. They might remember if Loew was on the tour bus when it pulled out of the Village.

"Jack?"

"Give me ten," he said as he began his search.

The first story that popped up was a feature from *The Clarion-Ledger*, Mississippi's largest newspaper, dated January 1991. The head: A Decade Later, Questions Linger in Tell Car Death.

Jack shifted in his chair to ward off a jab to his ribs.

Tell had been driving south from Nashville to his home in Gulfport when his Camaro Z28 spun out of control in the De Soto National Forest. It struck a tree and Tell, who wasn't wearing a seatbelt, was thrown into the windshield and killed instantly. Though the Forrest Country Sheriff's Department ruled it an accidental death, suspicions remained. Back in '81, a tow-truck driver told *The Clarion-Ledger* that Tell's front tire had torn clear off.

Molly ducked in. "Can't it wait?"

"Listen to this. Victor Loew ran the career of a singer who was killed back in '81 in an accident similar to the one I had. And the guy who messed with the Subaru was likely in New York the night Katy was killed.

"I've never done a story like this in my life. Medgar Wells might want it, but it would serve them right if I sent it to *The Times*."

"So much for magnanimity. Does revenge really suit you?"

"Oh, I could make it fit really well."

She walked to the kitchen. "I'm serving."

"Let me make one more call. I've got another lead."

A minute later, he had the phone number for the Tennessee Department of Agriculture bureau that issued licenses to manufacture hemp to make CBD products.

Dinner over, the dishes done, Jack was back at the kitchen counter, sketching out the flow of his story. Wearing his floppy socks, her feet on the big ottoman, tea on the end table, Molly was working *the Times of London* crossword puzzle with a Geo Strategic pen. She had earned a lazy night. Up before dawn, calling Switzerland, calling East Africa, a former client in Rome had contacted her with a possible assignment. A night of nothing was a reward. Jack proposed they nestle in next to each other and watch Edward G. Robinson play a Norwegian farmer.

"This story could take a while, though," he said over her laptop screen. "It has potential as a great long-form feature, the kind *The Observer* used to do so well. A discarded young woman. Talented, determined. Murder, not suicide. A song stolen, a dream dashed. Who knew what?"

Molly said, "Murder, Jack?"

"And why go after Tell? Was he going to come clean? I'm not there yet…"

She went back to her puzzle, but realized Jack was staring at her.

"Something's on your mind," she said. "Tell me."

He stood. "Thanks, Molly. That's all. Just thanks. Without you, I don't know…"

"Sit next to me, sweetheart," she said, tapping the sofa.

Down in Nashville, time fled for Jebby Stuart as he studied, books spread across the desk, yellow and blue markers on hand. He had forgotten about dinner, and when he looked up, the office was empty—a starry night pressed against the 14th-floor windows. He took the elevator to the garage beneath the glass-and-steel tower that was home to Lash, Hollenbeck and Rye.

As if to symbolize his dual role as law student and intern at one of the city's most prominent firms, Jebby wore a gray suit, dress shirt, tie and Nike kicks. Suitcase swinging at his side, he walked through silence with an athlete's grace, passing the few remaining parked cars.

He didn't see the man who hit him on the side with his company-issued Glock 17.

Jebby fell to his knees, but didn't collapse entirely. So the man hit him again and Jebby landed face-first on the concrete, fracturing his nose. He bled profusely.

Vic Loew took his briefcase and wallet, stealing the latter to make it appear a mere robbery. But when Nashville PD found the emptied briefcase tossed in an alley off Rosa Parks Boulevard, they knew the perpetrator was after more than money.

It was Arthur Lash himself who pressed the police to look into Loew. Young Jebby, he told media, "was a very fine student-athlete, much beloved at the University of Tennessee. At my insistence, our Jebby visited the senior Loew up in Oak Hill in order to clarify an issue we have taken under consideration. Mr. Loew, it must be said, declined young Jebby's gentle attention, but clearly his attendance was noted…"

The Metropolitan Nashville Police Department was somewhat dismayed to discover a member of the Davidson County Sheriff's Office, Sgt. Rhett Tackett, had leaked details of an ongoing investigation to *The Observer*. Metro Police requested that the sheriff in neighboring Wilson County send a patrol car to the Wilson Bank & Trust.

Loew hadn't turned up for work.

Nor was he at his home, a log cabin on six acres in Goodlettsville, paid for, no doubt, with funds supplied by his father.

Arthur Lash called Suzi Epstein-Lee to inform her that among the papers that were stolen from his intern were documents related to Lash, Hollenbeck and Rye's work on behalf of Giancarlo Fiorello.

Suzi called Jack. He and Molly were at an Italian restaurant they enjoyed south of Canal, about a mile from home. He had made a reservation; "a quiet corner, please." The hostess seated them with Jack's back to the fireplace. He could see the flames dance in Molly's eyes.

"It's Suzi," said Jack, picking up his phone.

Molly unrolled her napkin. "You'd better take it."

Suzi explained.

"Is Jebby all right?" Jack asked.

He will be, said Suzi. Already out of the hospital. "CCTV shows Loew entering and exiting the garage around the time Stuart clocked out. No one can find him."

"That makes sense, doesn't it? He's running. Did he really think he could scare off your guys?"

"It's probably nothing, Jack, but now Loew has your address. He knows where you live."

"Noted," said Jack. He looked at Molly and shrugged.

Suzi said, "Excuse me, Jack, but you're awfully blasé about this. Didn't you say you think this guy might've killed Katy? In New York?"

"Yeah. Forty years ago," he replied. "Listen, maybe I should call you back. I'm with Molly. It's busy in here."

She said fine. "Be careful, Jack."

He thanked her and sent her Molly's regards.

"What was that about?" Molly asked.

"The guy who ran me off the road stole some documents from Suzi and Henry's guys in Nashville."

Jack scanned the menu. He already knew what he wanted: a frittata with broccoli rabe and sweet sausage.

"And?"

"They can't find him."

Alarmed, she said, "Jack? Did Suzi say you should be concerned?"

"Vic Loew isn't one for clear thinking, but he has to know coming 900 miles to hassle me doesn't end his problems. Everything is documented now. His father ripped off Katy. He ripped off other composers. The Loews are collecting royalties for work the father didn't do, songs he didn't write. The son is probably frantic to protect that income stream. Traveling to New York won't help."

They placed their order. Jack dipped a piece of focaccia into olive oil flavored with cherry peppers.

Molly wasn't placated. "Come to Rome with me, Jack."

RFP approved, funding secured, she was heading out tomorrow. Just like that.

He said, "I have a few things I need to do—"

"If you're in danger—"

"Oh, please. I should flee to Rome… Well, it's an exotic idea, isn't it?"

"You'll be safe. You can write from anywhere. You've said that."

"Can't. I have a date tomorrow. With a woman. Be jealous."

"I'm not discounting your appeal, Jack, but with the stitches and the lumps and the wheezing—"

"And the limping."

"The limping."

"You know, old used cars are popular with a certain kind of consumer..."

She held his hand. "Be careful. We need you, Katy and me."

Jack put Molly's luggage in the town car's trunk.

"Dag Hammarskjöld Plaza," she told the driver. She would spend the morning at Geo Strategic Communications before heading to JFK.

Downy flakes stuck to the car's roof and windshield. Jack thought the snow wouldn't linger, but already a crew was at work on the east side of Broadway near City Hall, sweeping, salting.

As the driver waited, Jack and Molly stole a kiss.

"Let Suzi handle things now. See the doctor, get better."

"Molly, it's OK. Really." In his hoodie, he shivered. Snow gathered in his mismatched hair.

"You were never in danger as a rock critic," she said.

At Lollapalooza, a bossy stage manager pushed him down a flight of stairs, and Jack landed hard on his tailbone. In Denver, a Whitney Houston impersonator kissed him on the mouth. Her boyfriend came at Jack in a rage. Fortunately, he tripped and fell face-first into the rail beneath the bar.

The driver waited dutifully.

"I love you, Jack."

"I love you more."

She kissed him tenderly on his bruised cheek.

The town car slipped into traffic to circle toward Park Row to the FDR Drive. Soon, Molly would see ice floes on the East River.

Jack showered, changed the bandage on his head and popped a lone acetaminophen tablet. As he shaved, he studied his bruises. Discoloration aside, he almost seemed himself again. An aged human sparked by purpose had a youthful light in his eyes.

He dressed for the weather—his long topcoat over a heavy sweater and jeans, stocking cap. He found an old pair of Timberland boots in the back of a closet. He hated to wear them—the weight pulled on his back—but he had a bit of walking to do today, so what the hell. If all went well, he would be back home with a new laptop and new information well before dinner time, especially if Bernadette Tell returned his call.

He and Mary Donegal had agreed to meet at a Vietnamese restaurant equidistant between his home and 1PP. On the slow walk over, through Foley Square, red notebook in his pocket, he thumbed a phone number.

Don Emerson answered.

"Don, it's Jack Fiorello."

They exchanged pleasantries. It was snowing in Princeton. Freshmen were picking courses for the Spring semester. Winter recess begins on Friday.

Jack said, "Don, do you have a family lawyer?"

Emerson said no. "Why?"

"A couple of things."

Jack looked at the New York State Supreme Court Building. He saw Henry Fonda kicked down the steps as "Twelve Angry Men" came to its end. He heard the soaring trumpet in the theme for TV's "The Defenders." Suddenly, the world was in black and white.

"You might want to get a lawyer to look into a man named Victor Loew in Nashville." Jack spelled the last name. "Loew knows we know Katy wrote a song he produced for an artist named Grady Tell. He and Tell registered it under their names. It's one of the songs you've been paying BMI to protect: 'That Didn't Last Too Long.' Tell recorded it under a different title, but it's the same song."

Jack waited as Emerson made his notes.

"The song was the B side to a big hit, so somebody earned, Don."

"This is—"

"Terrible," Jack interrupted. "Katy trusted this guy and he ripped her off. And not just your sister. He owes many songwriters, Don. Go get him."

"Do I need a lawyer in the music industry? Can you recommend someone?"

"Maybe it's better if you go your own way. It's a family matter. But if you're in a bind, I've got someone who can point you right." He gave him Suzi's name and number.

"I was going to say it's unbelievable, Jack. After all these years…"

"I'm running around today. But let me know how it goes, OK?" said Jack. "Good luck."

Emerson thanked him as they rang off.

Jack found he was standing directly in front of the restaurant.

He peered through the glass and saw a beefy policewoman in blue who was made beefier by her bulletproof vest. She had chestnut hair and, as she looked at Jack looking at her, a bright, winning smile.

When he entered, she gestured for him to sit. They were in the corner of the small, mirrored room.

"You were watching the world go by?" he asked.

"You'll never see a cop who's alone sit back to the door."

They shook hands. Jack removed his topcoat and hat.

"What happened to your face? Your head?"

"I was ill-treated," Jack replied as he sat. "My ribs took the worst of it."

"You look older than the pictures I found online," she teased.

"Well, there's no way I could be younger, right? But, yeah, getting older is where this whole thing started."

They both ordered phở. The rice noodles and hot broth were perfect for a frigid day.

"Jack, before we begin, I'm single and ready to mingle, but married men are a no-go." The word "single" came out sort of like "shingle."

He told her about Molly. "So we're smooth, right?"

"Abso. My dad thinks Jack G. is the coolest guy ever. Me, I can't believe that's a real job."

It used to be… "Mary, I've come across some information that I'm thinking NYPD needs to know. Can I run it by you and see if you think it's a thing?"

Donegal nodded. She was disappointed. She wasn't ready to go for a 65-year-old rock critic, but she was thinking she might've enjoyed the chase.

As he showed her the photo of Katy in Washington Square Park, Jack told Donegal what he had learned.

"And I talked to Grady Tell's daughter," he added. "She said she always thought her dad was killed. Turns out he had second thoughts about ripping off Katy and the other songwriters. He told Loew. Is it melodramatic to say they succeeded in getting rid of him in the same way they failed to get rid of me?"

She said, "Let's stay on point, Jack G. So you're thinking this guy Loew was here and he killed your friend Katy."

"That's about it." He dipped basil leaves into his steaming broth. "It's circumstantial—"

"You think?"

"I'm saying it's worth starting a conversation. Based on what I've found out, the case isn't really closed."

"You want to be able to write that you, Jack G. Fiorello, is responsible for the department re-opening the case."

"No. No. Jesus. But, yes, I want the case reopened. Can't you exhume the body or something? See if there were bruises that indicate she was wrestled up the stairs and across the roof?"

"Jack, you watch too much TV."

"Probably. But this Vic Loew is a killer."

"Volume…" she warned. The restaurant was steps from the courthouse. At least half of its lunchtime customers were lawyers.

"Sorry," Jack said sheepishly.

"Tell you what: Write a memo, send it to me and I'll ask around. No promises."

They ate in silence, save for the slurping.

"You ought to know, Mary, that my time is up at *The Observer*. Aged out. No more weekly columns."

"Really? My dad will be bummed. Are you going to retire?"

"I am not. We'll see what happens after I do this story."

"But not for *The Observer*?"

"Probably not," he said, "so do me a favor. Slow-play it until I get it together."

"If I push this up the chain, I'm not responsible if it leaks."

"Granted. Looks like I owe you another lunch," Jack said.

"Make another mix for my dad and we're even."

Deal struck, they shook hands.

Chivalry not entirely dead, he walked Donegal toward 1PP until she decided to peel off. Then he turned around and started toward Eldridge Guitars. It was time for A.A. Carpenter to own up.

The guitar shop was about a mile away. Rather than hail a cab, Jack decided to walk along the Bowery before turning east. Moving gingerly, he pulled his stocking cap down over his ears. He remembered how, at a Bridge School concert in Mountain View, California, one late October, his fingers froze around his pencil as he waited for Metallica to do an unplugged set. At Coachella 2012, it was so cold in the desert that Jack stood dangerously close to the red coals of a barbecue pit while the Black Keys closed out the Friday night bill.

He blew into his hands as he crossed Grand Street. Though the snow had stopped, the sky was a dismal gray. Nightfall threatened and it wasn't much past two o'clock. He foresaw ice on lower Broadway and, by the time rush hour began, commuters slipping and careening as if on a frozen rink. Thoughts of how to move Carpenter to where he needed him to be had been overtaken by his eagerness to get out of the December cold.

At the guitar store, he looked past the instruments in the window toward the counter.

Vic Loew was barking at Carpenter. The big, bearded man looked terribly afraid.

Chapter Sixteen

Jack retreated. He pulled out his phone. Who to call? Stay calm, Jack. Stay calm…

An admin put him through to Suzi.

"He's at Eldridge Guitars. Loew. Vic Loew."

"Where are you?"

"In a Starbucks across the street. Big window. You must know detectives. Right?"

"A few."

"Nashville PD wants him."

"Get out of there, Jack."

"Hold on. He's leaving. He's walking away…"

He watched as Loew yanked the music store door and stormed past the coffee shop, all wiry and nasty and way under-dressed in a well-worn Carhartt coat and jeans. Head down in a ball cap, he blasted north along Allen Street.

"Remember," Jack added, "he knows New York. At least he did four decades ago."

Stepping carefully back into the cold, Jack watched as Loew disappeared.

Suzi told him she'd be in touch.

Collar up, Jack put the phone in his pocket and, crunching rock salt underfoot, crossed toward Eldridge Guitars.

Way in back, someone was playing Dimebag Darrell riffs, stomping a Crybaby pedal. Jack kept his eye on the dusty velvet curtain behind the counter. Soon, it rippled and parted.

"Oh great," moaned Carpenter. The big man wore a black hoodie with the Florida Georgia Line logo crossing the zipper.

Hat in pocket, pencil in hand, Jack opened his notebook. "I saw him," he said.

Carpenter looked at the scar on the side of Jack's head. "I guess you did."

"I saw him here. It's too late," Jack told him. "He can't stop what's coming."

Now the guitarist in back was playing the snarling riffs from Pantera's "5 Minutes Alone."

"Why are you telling me? Tell him."

"NYPD will handle him," Jack said. "I've got questions for you. Tell your side—

for the record."

"My side of what?"

"Swanson Seagull. 'Our Last Morning Coffee.' You didn't write that song."

"You can't know that."

"I talked to Babs White. I have a copy of her original demo. Segal says you told the band you wrote it. The stolen copyright made you decent money."

"Made more for Loew," Carpenter muttered as he fussed with a tray of picks on the countertop.

Confirmed: Victor Loew stole it.

"What do you need?" Carpenter asked finally.

"You told Victor Loew Katy had a song worth stealing."

"Didn't have to. I'd sent him the Bitter End tape. He knew what it was."

"You'd gone from hustling in the Village to Swanson Seagull's backup band. Did Loew get you that gig?"

"He knew I could play. We stayed in touch. Why not?"

"After you knew he ripped off Katy."

"Swanson Seagull was steady work. I couldn't undo what happened to her."

Jack said, "On your word, she disrupted her life and moved to Nashville—and you knew it was likely she would be hustled."

"She was already fucked. Grady cut the track even before she got to town." He shrugged. "Happens. Nashville could've worked for her. She had the talent. Get over it, move on, dig in."

"Was there anything about Katy that told you she would just move on?" Jack cringed as a blast of feedback came from the rear of the store. "You saw her when she returned, didn't you?"

"Of course I did. She stomped into my place and just about bit my head off. The next night, I was showcasing at Kenny's, open-mike night. I looked up and she's standing square in front of me. In the spotlight. Her shadow on me and my guitar." Carpenter shook his head. "That stare of hers. Not a word. She just stared. Man."

"So you knew she would confront Grady Tell."

"Wasn't hard to figure. She was waitressing at the Lone Star. They couldn't miss each other."

"And Vic Loew was here with Grady Tell," Jack led.

"I had no fuckin' idea who Vic Loew was. His father, yeah. Him, no."

"If Katy confronts Tell at the Lone Star, the whole thing is out in the open. Nashville knows Victor Loew is a thief."

From the back came gentle chords on an acoustic guitar: the chording in E that opens Led Zeppelin's "Ramble On."

"What did Vic Loew just tell you?"

Carpenter scoffed. "Same thing you did. I'm fucked. If you write your story, the old man is going to tell everybody I delivered songs for him to steal. That I was the pipeline."

"Were you?"

"I told you. I tipped him off when I heard a good song. I never told him to claim he wrote them."

Jack said, "Why go that route?"

"What route? 'Here's a good song. Push it.'"

"More like 'steal it.'"

"Why are you dumping on me? Victor Loew made a lot more. A lot more. And he did it, I don't know, a couple dozen times."

Thirty-two, thought Jack. "You should've told me that straight up."

"Why? So I can have Vic Loew on my ass too?"

Jack didn't reply. The guitarist had stopped playing deep in the back of the store. He heard footsteps.

A girl, maybe 10 or 11 years old, appeared. As she slipped back into her down coat, she looked at Carpenter, said, "Thanks, mister" and, pulling mittens from her pockets, left the store.

"Where is Loew staying?"

Carpenter shook his head. "He's halfway to somewhere else, if he's smart."

"Anyone tell you he's smart?" Jack asked, as he put his notebook in his coat pocket.

Back in his Tribeca apartment, Jack sipped sparkling water at the kitchen counter. What's next? With the help of Bernadette Tell, he would contact surviving members of the Grady Tell Band to find out if Katy confronted him at the Lone Star. They might confirm Vic Loew was in New York when Katy was killed.

Wrote Jack in his notebook: How much did Loew make on Katy's song? On Swanson Seagull's hit? The others?

Get a country icon on the record about how damaging song theft is to emerging artists. Willie? Kristofferson?

"Any recommendations, Katy?"

As he washed up, Suzi called. Nashville police had interviewed Victor Loew, who said he had no way of contacting his son. At the Wilson Bank & Trust, the police were told Loew didn't carry a cellphone. If he had a friend in New York, none of his colleagues knew who it could be.

"Anybody ask Victor Loew if he still has Katy's tapes?"

"Jack, please. Focus. Don't be flip."

"Suzi, the front door is locked."

"Where's Molly?" she asked.

Jack looked at the clock on the laptop screen. It was coming up on 8 p.m. "Somewhere over the Atlantic. On her way to Rome."

"Let's talk in the morning," Suzi suggested. "And please don't do anything we'll regret."

He dug his sweats and a hoodie out of the laundry bin. As he slipped into his beat-up old Vans, he thought of Rome: the little restaurant he and Molly savored together off the Via Corso, holding hands on the stroll back to the hotel, a cobblestone street, stars sprinkled in the indigo sky, everything but an accordionist. He recalled how they made love, the curtains fluttering at the open windows, the night air stroking their bodies.

All joys Katy Shayne was denied.

Katy Shayne and the Black Canyon City Band. He had transferred the fantasy to memory and could see and hear her and the band as if they had performed right in front of him. Blistering set; great tunes well-played and sung by a charismatic singer. Katy was the full package.

Jack opened his eyes.

He decided to make *spaghetti cacio e pepe*, as if the meal would transport him to Molly's side. He put on the water to boil. Holiday films had begun to take over the retro-minded movie channels, but it was too soon for sleigh bells and jingles. He pulled the Book Review from last Sunday's *New York Times* and skimmed it until it was time to toast the pepper.

He ate at the kitchen counter, spooling the spaghetti around his fork, a generous glass of Barolo his companion. A simple salad of arugula and red onion finished the meal.

"Sated," he said as he closed the book section.

Cleaning up, Jack slipped the Parmigiano Reggiano rind into the plastic bag, then brought the cutting board to the trash can, scraping away bits of onion.

"Phew," said Jack as a foul scent wafted toward him.

He lifted the trash bag and tied it tight. He decided to dump it now rather than risk a leak by morning.

"I'll be right back," he said to no one.

He opened the door.

And there was Vic Loew.

Wearing a sickly grin, Loew was holding his gun at his side.

The door slammed shut behind Jack.

All Jack could manage was: "You're too late."

"Not to deal with you." Wild-eyed, he took a step forward.

"You killed Katy. Threw her off the roof."

"Now I'm about to kill you."

Jack flung the trash bag at him.

The gun dropped to the carpeted floor.

As Loew groped to retrieve it, Jack jumped on his back, a knee aimed at his spine.

Loew rolled, kicked at Jack.

Jack shoved Loew's head toward the floor. And then he stood as quickly as his body would allow. Fumbling his keys, he hurried toward the stairwell in the elevator lobby.

Loew caught up with him as Jack spun toward the marble stairs. Grabbing Jack by the hood, he yanked him back to the landing. Loew threw a looping blow to Jack's tender ribs.

As he fell, Jack yowled in pain.

Sensing the weakness, Loew kicked Jack in the ribs again. Then he kicked him again.

As he lifted his leg a third time, Jack reached up and shoved the bottom of Loew's boot. Loew stumbled backward.

And then tumbled over the waist-high railing, falling into open space.

Jack heard but didn't see. Loew slammed repeatedly into the iron railings as he dropped eight stories to the ground floor.

When Jack managed to stand, pulling himself up by the rail, he looked down. Loew was a bloody heap far, far below.

Then Jack passed out.

Lightheaded, in pain, he was on his feet when uniformed NYPD arrived.

"What happened?" they asked with steely detachment.

Surrounded by neighbors who crowded the vestibule and the stairs, Jack suggested the cops come to his apartment.

Better to wait for the detectives, he was told.

Nevertheless, Jack limped away, wheezing, his hand on the wall for support. As his ribs rebelled in pain, his right leg began to go numb. He could taste blood.

He saw Loew's gun in the corridor. He pointed toward it to the uniform who had followed him.

Jack recovered from two broken ribs, a bruised kidney, and countless interviews, the latter resulting in stories that were variations on "Rock Critic Fights Off, Kills Musical Intruder." *The New York Post* insisted on sending a photographer to the hospital.

"What a sad sack," Jack said when he saw the picture in the paper. "My hair. I look like I fell into a lawn mower."

"The notebook and pencil," said Molly. "Nice touch."

She had hopscotched home from Rome with stopovers in Paris and Newfoundland. She was unaware that the man she had ridden the hospital elevator with was Lee Reinhard, Jack's former editor. Thoroughly professional, she accepted his handshake when Jack introduced them. Sensing their need for time alone, Reinhard left quickly, though not before mentioning that Medgar Wells still wanted to talk about what happened.

"Thank him for me," Jack replied, saying nothing more.

He had been home now for three days, up and about for two. In the building, he was a macabre hero: A man of bad intent had entered, violating the neighbors' sense of security. The gun-wielding stranger deserved to be punished. But killed? In our stairwell?

"I'd rather not," said Jack when Mrs. Mewalal asked him to autograph the photo in *the Post*.

The super took care to wipe away blood and every bit of bone.

Jack had yet to reveal to Molly what had happened in any greater detail than he gave the New York papers and *the Tennessean*. "When you're ready…" she told him.

Now, Jack and Molly sat together on the sofa. "I'm ready," he said, his ribs bandaged, ice pack on his bruised wrist.

Molly put down her magazine.

Jack said, "So I had just finished dinner…"

A few minutes later, Molly said, with a whimper, "I could've lost you, Jack."

They held hands in silence. Then Jack said, "It's some kind of ugly justice,

I guess, with Vic Loew. Not really, though, and way too late."

He gritted his teeth and hoisted himself from the sofa.

"Nothing's in the way now," he said. "Katy's story can be told. Her music needs to be heard.

"I got to go to work."

His new laptop awaited.

Chapter Seventeen

On the morning of Valentine's Day Eve, Jack and Molly went to the local Le Pain Quotidien, where they enjoyed cappuccinos, soft-boiled eggs and a bread basket. Jack watched as Molly read a hard copy of the article he had slugged "A Song for Katy Shayne."

When Molly finished, she had tears in her eyes.

"It's wonderful, Jack. It's riveting. Really."

He nodded. "It's the damnedest thing, isn't it? Thirty-five hundred words. Nothing like *The Observer* style." *Vanity Fair* had purchased the piece.

"The New York City police are going to re-open the case?"

"So they say."

"We should celebrate with Suzi and Henry," she said.

"I owe them, for sure," Jack replied. He was mangling his soft-boiled egg. Little pieces of shell dotted the tabletop. "But now that you've seen it, let me send it to Suzi. She told me Henry knows a couple of people out in Hollywood. You never know."

Molly sipped her cappuccino and dabbed away a foamy mustache. Morning traffic flowed south toward the World Trade Center Memorial.

Molly had food-shopped at a local market: not much, some things to nosh while they reminisced. As she set the kitchen counter, she stopped again to admire the bouquet of bright African daisies Jack placed in a pitcher. "Beautiful flowers," she told him.

"Beautiful wife," he replied.

"Jack, you're such a romantic," said Suzi from the kitchen, where she was nibbling from the buffet. "Who knew?" She wore an electric blue miniskirt over swirly yellow tights.

Sweet kora music from Senegal, courtesy of Femi and his Chambers Street table, floated overhead.

Now, the entry buzzer buzzed. Marta Pacheco's face filled the intercom's little screen.

"Come on up," Jack said. He slipped into his double-breasted blazer and left it unbuttoned over his shirt and jeans.

Molly, in a black turtleneck and a bright patterned skirt, suggested he wait in the hall.

Soon, the elevator opened, and Marta stepped out, wrapped in a lovely burgundy coat and soft gray hat. She smiled hesitantly yet accepted Jack's embrace.

He noticed immediately that she was wearing the turquoise earrings she and Katy shared decades ago.

At that moment, the other elevator opened, and out stepped Don Emerson, whose puffy North Face coat didn't quite cover his suit jacket.

"Welcome," Jack said, stepping toward him.

He didn't so much shake Jack's hand as hold it between his palms. "Thank you. Thank you."

Stepping back, Jack said, "Have you two met?"

"So long ago," Don said as they hugged.

"You were a boy," Marta recalled. "You were like a moth around a flame with Katy."

"Oh, how I adored her."

Marta smiled. "I did, too."

Waiting by the door, Molly welcomed their guests.

Jack introduced Marta to Suzi and Henry—"our friends, and without whom…" he said. "Don, you've spoken to Suzi."

"You're not like I pictured you," Don said.

"I like that, Mr. Emerson. Keep it up."

In a white shirt, tie, blue blazer and khakis, Henry took the coats and brought them to the bedroom.

Though Jack gestured toward the living room, Marta and Don lingered near the kitchen. Molly had opened a Pinot Gris, and on the counter were figs, olives, crispy raisin bread, membrillo, a strawberry jam, and several cheeses. As she sat, she said, "I have a quiche if you're hungry. It won't take more than a few minutes to heat."

Marta was staring at Don. "I'm not sure I see her in you," she said. "Around the eyes, perhaps. The nose."

"Well, I'm just a creaky old man now," he replied, "but Katy would have aged as you have, Marta. You are as lovely as I recall."

Nah, thought Jack. At 65, Katy would be a samurai with a black Fender Jaguar, a no-bullshit terror, an Americana queen, a—

"You know, Don," Marta said, "praise did not roll off your sister's tongue."

"The default position in the Emerson household was to criticize. But she loved you, Marta. You were her first true love," he replied.

"Don," Jack said, "can you do Katy's famous stare? The one that buckled knees? Made grown men whimper?"

Don furrowed his brow, leaned in and narrowed his eyes. Jack, Molly and Marta laughed.

"No, I guess not," he said.

Jack proposed a toast. "To Katy. For bringing us together. And for her music."

After a sip or two, Don said, "And to Jack. We all know what he's done for us and for my sister."

Jack bowed his head. As Molly beamed, Suzi threw him a playful kiss.

He said, "There are a few things, Don, you should think about. Believe it or not, Victor Loew—"

"The song thief," Marta said.

"Not that he's copping to it. But he has a storage space filled with contracts and a lot of stuff. Tapes too. Don, it's not my place, but if I were you, I'd get whatever tapes Loew has of Katy. Demos, showcases, whatever."

He looked at Suzi, who nodded in agreement.

"There's a couple of guys down in Goodlettsville, Tennessee. Milt Klinger and his son Paul. Good people. They run a recording studio, Blunderbuss.

See what they can do with whatever you get, the MP3s I sent you and the tape Marta gave me of the Bitter End show."

"Like what?"

"See if they can be cleaned up and made ready for release."

"You mean for sale?"

Jack said, "One step at a time, Don. They're more than forty years old, in mono and on dime-store cassettes. But find out if you can get the best tracks to a quality sufficient for Soundcloud or Bandcamp. If so, post the best. When the *Vanity Fair* piece comes out, hire a publicist and get the labels to listen. Maybe a singer or two looking for good songs will be interested."

Henry said, "Don, Marta, if I can help in any way, don't hesitate."

Don said, "I don't know what to say. Do you think it can work? I mean, do people care?"

"If we care, they'll care," Marta said. She tapped Don's hand.

Don sighed. "I don't know anyone anymore who knew Katy. She's forgotten."

"She'll be remembered soon," Molly said.

They all looked at Jack.

Jack was thinking ahead. He was going to see Spoon, Son Lux and Kaitlyn Aurelia Smith at the Beacon Theatre on Tuesday night. He loved those artists and their music loved him.

Weird, though, to buy a ticket. He hadn't realized they were so expensive...

And then you have to stand on line to get in?

"The thing is," Jack said, "you guys know best. Whatever Katy wants, do. The most important is to let people hear her music."

Soon, Marta and Don were seated at the counter, small plates and cutlery at hand, bottled water joining the Italian white. As Molly nudged the serving tray toward them, Suzi eavesdropped, elbows on gray marble, her chin cupped in her hands.

Marta declined. "I don't eat much these days."

As Don began to make a plate, Molly said, "Marta, if you wouldn't mind, would you tell me about Katy? Don, would you too?"

Jack understood. He had told Molly about Katy Shayne as a musician from her teen years until her disappointment in Nashville. Both Marta and Don had given him a sense of her, but they had been speaking to a journalist. Molly wanted to know what she was like as a girl and a young woman.

As they spoke, Jack listened. He heard their bittersweet laughs; soon, Don and Marta began to question each other: "I didn't know that. Tell me more." When Don mentioned the trip to Hoboken to buy Katy's first good guitar, Marta said, "Your mother gave her strength."

"I can tell that my mom would have loved you too," Don replied.

"You know, I often wondered if, in time, Katy and I would have become good, good friends. Best friends." Eyes moist, Marta pressed a hand to her chest. "I have a feeling of peace. In my heart, there is peace."

In mine, too, thought Jack G. Fiorello.

Author's Note

A Song for Katy Shayne is a work of fiction, though it contains several events I experienced as the Rock & Pop Critic of the *Wall Street Journal*. Any criticism of the fictional *New National Observer* and its personnel in the novel should not be interpreted as commentary on my many years with the *Journal*. I had the best time as its chief rock music critic, and I have nothing but respect and affection for my former colleagues.

Throughout the novel, there are references to songs written by Katy Shayne. In fact, they were written by me way back in the era in which *A Song for Katy Shayne* is set. I never finished "Looking for the Girl," but "That Didn't Last Too Long," "Celia Remains, "Secrets of a Shy Girl" – whose actual title is "The Girl I Remember – "Born Outsider," "I'm Gone" (not mentioned by name herein) and "You Can't Go Back" – actual title "The Cradle Will Rock" – were all part of my repertoire in the Greenwich Village clubs. I last played them in public in Los Angeles in 2013. (I have a tape of that show, but I've never listened to it.) All are properly copyrighted and registered. If you have any interest in hearing them, let me know. I'm sure Katy wouldn't mind.

About the Author

Jim Fusilli is the author of 11 novels, including *The Price You Pay*, *The Mayor of Polk Street,* and its predecessor, *Narrows Gate*. His short fiction appears in numerous anthologies, including The Best American Mystery Stories. He's also host and executive producer of the popular podcast *Writers at Work,* featuring interviews with top authors about the joys, heartaches, challenges, and satisfaction of the creative writing process.

The former Rock & Pop Critic for *The Wall Street Journal,* Jim's book *Pet Sounds* is his tribute to Brian Wilson and the Beach Boys' classic album. He lives in New York City.

AUTHOR WEBSITE:
www.jimfusilli.com

SOCIAL MEDIA HANDLES:
Facebook: Jim Fusilli
Bluesky: @jimfusilli.bsky.social

Also by Jim Fusilli

NOVELS:
The Mayor of Polk Street
Narrows Gate
Billboard Man
Road to Nowhere
Marley Z and the Blood-Stained Violin
Hard, Hard City
Tribeca Blues
A Well-Known Secret
Closing Time

NON-FICTION:
Pet Sounds